THE GIRLS OF CANBY HALL

OUR ROOMMATE IS
MISSING

Emily Chase

SCHOLASTIC INC.
New York Toronto London Auckland Sydney Tokyo

*For Martha, with love
and gratitude always.*

ISBN 0-590-32850-6

12 11 10 9 8 7 6 5 4 3 2   4 5 6 7/8

Printed in the U.S.A.   01

THE GIRLS OF CANBY HALL

OUR ROOMMATE IS
MISSING

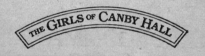

THE GIRLS OF CANBY HALL

Roommates
Our Roommate Is Missing
You're No Friend of Mine
Keeping Secrets

CHAPTER ONE

Shelley's disappearance didn't register on her two roommates, Faith and Dana, all at once. Not only were they slow to realize that she was really gone, they even laughed about it.

The three girls, Dana Morrison, Faith Thompson, and Michelle Hyde (always called Shelley) had safely survived their first half-year in boarding school together. The same differences that had caused them endless heartache in the beginning had welded them into a trio that giggled more than glared.

Dana was the first one back to their room that Sunday night. Her first act, of course, had been to shrug out of the trim, knitted dress that had been her uniform for the special Parent-Alumnae Weekend just past. She couldn't get into her pajamas fast enough. The peppermint-striped pajamas with the feet attached had been a Christmas joke from her mother. Little did her fashionable mother, who was a buyer for a well-known New York store, realize that the drafty floors of Baker House would make those built-in booties the envy of the entire fourth floor. After changing, she unpacked the treats her mother had brought for the three of them. Just as she finished, Faith dragged in.

Faith leaned against the door and slid her camera strap off with a groan.

"What a day," she sighed. "I must have shot a million pictures this weekend. I have peered through that lens finder until I am black in the face."

Dana chuckled. Her tall, black roommate was so open — even humorous — about their differences that Dana often wanted to just grab her for a hug. There had been a time, at the beginning, when these same differences had threatened to make Room 407 the Canby Hall equivalent of Antarctica, with each of them trying to freeze the others out. Now, Room 407 was the greatest place in Baker House, if not the entire school.

Not that they had managed to do it by themselves. Left to their own resources, it could only have gone from worse to horrendous. Alison Cavanaugh, the dorm houseparent, had performed magic over tea and cookies in her penthouse apartment. More had come from that night than just the friendship among the roommates, Dana thought. Living away from home would have been pretty bleak without someone as wise and calm as Alison to turn to. Just seeing Alison's friendly wave from down a hall was somehow reassuring.

Faith, still wriggling her shoulders, looked around the room with a frown. "Where's Shel?" she asked. Even after the long day just past, Faith looked fantastic. Although she wasn't into high-fashion clothes, Faith always managed to achieve a smooth style of her own. Her medium-length Afro emphasized the brilliance of her expressive eyes. And those eyes were for real. Dana had never known anyone so clear-eyed and honest about herself and the world as Faith was.

"Shelley," Dana announced, "is lost. Gone. Disappeared like a puff of smoke." Dana's tone was airy as she adjusted the mustard jar that was threatening to take a flying leap off the lobster crate that they used as a coffee table.

Faith's tone was one of mock patience. "One loses one's mittens. One also loses one's pencil on final exam day. One can even lose a reputation. One does *not* lose a slightly overweight but nonetheless adorable roommate like our Shelley.

"Especially if there is food," she added, leaning hungrily over the lobster crate to examine Dana's display.

"That's what makes her disappearance so

really mysterious," Dana agreed. "I caught up with her between the art show and lunch and told her what Mom had brought us. I expected her to be waiting with her napkin under her chin on the dot of ten-thirty."

"Your mother is simply the greatest," Faith decided aloud. The selection of food on the lobster crate included the favorites of each of the girls. And their tastes were clearly as different as they were. Dana, tall, slender, and as stylish as the New York City she called home, was a hopeless addict of cream cheese and bagels. The oversized pretzels by the mustard jar were a taste that Faith had brought from her Washington, D.C., home. Her childhood, like the blazing hot mustard she preferred, had not been without pain. While peanut butter cookies with a chocolate kiss melted on the top didn't exactly spell Pine Bluff, Iowa, they did suggest the cozy warmth of Shelley's sheltered, small-town girlhood.

"Is it possible she has a reason for running late?" Dana asked. "This has hardly been a run-of-the-mill weekend."

Faith chuckled softly at Dana's understatement. Parent-Alumnae Weekend was one of the biggest events on the Canby Hall calendar. Every department had planned for it for weeks. Windows shone, and the halls were polished to a dangerous gleam. Everything possible had been arranged to make the school live up to the memories of its graduates and to live down the complaints that current students were writing home in their letters.

But no matter what the girls of Canby Hall might write home in the heat of anger, every student there was secretly proud to be a part of the old school that had stood on broad green acres since 1897. Each girl had stood beneath the portrait of Julia Canby in the immense entrance hall of Main Building. Julia Canby had been thirteen when the portrait was painted. Something in her wistful expression stirred a painful response in the heart of everyone who looked at her.

Her tragic early death the same year the portrait was painted had inspired her father to build Canby Hall on the land that would have been Julia's inheritance. The house in which Julia had grown up was now the residence of the headmistress, Patrice Allardyce. Julia must have warmed herself in the same shelter by the skating pond where the girls still gathered and patted the foals in the barnyard just as they did.

And it was no wonder that past graduates loved to return to walk the wooded paths and throw a fresh coin into the wishing pond. Many of them, like Faith and Shelley, had been students here only because old Horace Canby had set aside a scholarship fund when the school was built. He didn't want a school that catered only to girls of wealthy families. However they had come to Canby Hall, the older graduates shared a special love of the place. Dana saw more than one aging face glisten with tears as the choir sang the closing strains of the Canby Hall song.

But as pleasant as Parent-Alumnae Weekend was for the guests, it was almost an endurance test for the students. Every girl had a full schedule of assignments for the entire weekend.

The bulky camera equipment that Faith had deposited on the floor reflected most of the hours of her past two days. Her unerring eye for design and an instinct for human drama in photography had quickly established her as the star photographer for the *Canby Clarion*. Knowing that these pictures would not only be featured in the *Clarion* and the yearbook but would also be treasured by families for years, she had really stretched herself. The light had been weak under a storm-threatening sky. She was a little concerned about the quality of the outside shots through both days.

Dana had been assigned a place behind the massive Canby silver tea service in the hospitality parlor of Main Building. "Coffee or tea?" she had asked endlessly. "Lemon or milk?" *Coffee or tea? Lemon or milk? Sugar and cream?* The words marched through her mind as she smiled at the endless stream of chilled guests looking for comfort between events. She imagined that she must sound like a nodding black-crested parrot with her endless "Coffee or tea?"

As a consequence, neither Faith nor Dana had seen much of Shelley through the entire weekend. Faith had managed a few minutes with her mother and brother Richard on Sunday, and Dana had talked quite a while with her own mother, up from New York City. Shelley's parents hadn't been able to make the long, expensive trip from Iowa. Still, it was Shelley who spent the whole time with a guest. She had been the steady companion and hostess to Casey Flint's Aunt Edie from Boston.

Dana was a little confused as to how this had come about, but it was just like Shelley to find something kind to do for someone. Casey Flint was certainly not a person to worry about anyone else's feelings. When Casey learned that her own mother and father weren't coming for the weekend, she threw a world-class tantrum. She swore she wouldn't even be civil to the aunt who was coming up from Boston in her parents' place. She even tore her room apart and discarded everything in it that reminded her of her mother and father. Faith had taken the things and put them in her own closet, knowing Casey would regret the hasty action.

Casey had been the only loser. Every time

Dana saw Aunt Edie and Shelley, the older woman was beaming with delight and talking away with Shelley, as if they had known each other forever.

But the last train had left with lots of time for Shelley to get back to Baker House. By now the doors were locked for the night. Where could Shelley possibly be?

"Starvation makes me cranky," Faith announced after she had changed into her nightshirt and flannel robe. "I also have it on good authority that extended starvation is injurious to your health."

Then, because it was a game that the three of them played together, she reversed the meaning of "I Love My Love" and did it backward with Shelley's name.

"I unlove my *Shelley* with a *sneer* because she is so *slow*. She should eat *salamanders* and *spinach* and live in the *sink*."

"Oh, Faith," Dana protested. "You know that this isn't like Shelley at all. Could she have charmed Casey's Aunt Edie so thoroughly that she wasn't able to unload her? Could she be out there finding one more midnight marvel of Canby Hall to show off to her?"

In spite of her light words, Dana found her uneasiness growing. If nothing else, Shelley could be in really hot water if their dorm monitor happened to waken from her usual hibernation to do a bed check. Heather Blackburn was a nice enough girl but such a worrier about her responsibilities as monitor that she had usually exhausted herself long before anyone else had even thought about going to bed.

By eleven o'clock, Dana found herself struggling to control the little squiggle of worry that began just above her belt. It would have spiraled right up to her throat if she had let it. This was simply not like Shelley at all. She finally ate one bagel without tasting it. Faith had a single pretzel dipped in her hot mustard, and half-jokingly, they set off to go, as Faith put it, "Shel hunting."

The longer they looked and the more people they asked, the more Dana found herself concerned. No one could recall having seen Shelley all afternoon. As for herself, Dana last remembered Shelley and Casey's Aunt Edie cradling tea cups a little before noon. Back in their own room again, she and Faith frowned at each other.

Dana tried to think of all the things that might have happened to keep Shelley from getting back to the room. After all, Baker was an old building and there were only security lights on at night. What if Shelley had tripped on the stairs and fallen? Could she be in a bathroom somewhere with a cracked head?

"Talk about positive thinking," Faith rebuked her. "Maybe you should start a lending library of horrible thoughts."

But Dana noticed she was quick enough to

come along when Dana decided to check every place in the building where an accident like that could possibly happen.

Familiar places turned ghostly under the dim lights. The drapes of the study room stirred ominously, as if they concealed something hidden. The bathrooms all seemed to harbor strange sounds, erratic drips that sounded as if something unseen were sending a watery message in Morse code. The tiny kitchenette was the perfect setting for a Hitchcock movie, with the pilot lights glimmering eerily in the stove.

It was almost midnight as they stared through the slats of the venetian blinds from the darkness inside. Hall rules forbid lights on in rooms after midnight when there are classes the next day. The only glow in the room came from the dial of Shelley's alarm clock, an eerie light marking the minutes that were plunging Shelley deeper and deeper into trouble.

At least there was light beyond the window. Scraps of tired snow shone beneath the lamps that lined the circle drive in front of Baker Hall. A few brittle stars winked through the naked branches of the giant elms that marked the drive.

"I don't like this," Faith said for the umpteenth time. "How can I yell at her for not coming to our party when I can't even find her?"

"You checked every room on east?" Dana asked. Dana herself had checked the west wing, and every bed was filled.

Faith nodded. "I even found Alison's cat Doby wandering around and carried him up to Alison's room so I could check if Shelley were up there."

"And you're sure that Casey's aunt didn't stay over at the Inn? She might have gotten permission from somebody and invited Shelley as a guest."

Faith shook her head. "It should be on the sign-out sheet, and it's not. Anyway, Casey mentioned that her aunt was going back on the late train. 'Good riddance on the eight forty-eight' was how she put it." Faith frowned. "What if Shelley . . . ?"

They stared at each other for a long moment. Before the Christmas holiday Shelley had been really homesick for her boyfriend, Paul, back in Iowa. If someone wanted to run away, Parent-Alumnac Weekend would be the perfect time because there was so much confusion. And after all, a couple of months before, Casey Flint had not only *thought* of running away, she had actually *done* it. If Faith hadn't gone after her and talked her into trying again, she might be running still.

But Shelley wasn't Casey Flint.

Dana shook her head. "Not Shelley. You know, Faith, we have to make up our minds to report this to Alison."

Faith groaned and turned away from the window. Faith was always the last to give up on anything or anyone. Like her mother who was a social worker in Washington, D.C., Faith was all heart in spite of her flippant tongue.

The minute hand still sped on Shelley's clock as Dana tried to gear herself up for what they had to do. It wasn't as if Alison were an average housemother. She was a genuine, neat human being. She could be wise and calm and caring all at once, which is a little like patting your stomach and rubbing your head while you're on a whirling Ferris wheel.

"Okay," Faith said dully. "Gung and ho and all those active things."

Dana dragged herself to her feet. "I'm trying to forget that no matter what, this is going to end up with Shelley in trouble. I hate to see it happen to her. I love her, you know. She's very special."

"Special," Faith echoed, not meeting Dana's eyes. "But she's also too special to be in possible trouble without our making some effort to help."

"Now who's having horrible thoughts?" Dana challenged her.

Dana was almost at the door when she heard the faint sound vibrating through the ceiling.

"A phone," she whispered. "That's a phone ringing."

Faith's eyes narrowed as the sound came again. "Alison's penthouse is right above us here. That has to be her emergency phone."

Dana nodded. The switchboard was turned off at twelve o'clock, and even the pay phones were rigged not to work after midnight. It had to be the emergency phone in the housemother's apartment.

CHAPTER TWO

"**E**mergency," Faith repeated, almost under her breath. Yet even as softly as the word came, Dana was chilled by the horror that Faith managed to put into it.

Dana dropped her eyes and waited. During the months that they had been friends, she had only gradually learned about Faith's family. For one thing, Faith wasn't a chatterer. Although she was talkative enough, with a tart, wry wit that Dana loved, Faith seldom talked about herself. Almost all that Dana knew about Faith's feelings for her family had come from things Faith did rather than what she said.

Faith was a stubbornly careful student. Often hers was the last lamp to be put out in the study room down the hall. Shelley, like a restless hen with one chick still out of the nest, would rise on an elbow and complain, "Isn't that girl ever coming to bed?"

Faith always came, of course, but only after she was fully prepared for her classes. It was clear that Faith was devoted to her older sister Sarah, on full scholarship at George Washington University, and had no intention of making any less impressive a record than Sarah had.

As for her brother Richard, Faith couldn't walk through a store without lagging behind to stare at games and toys that an eleven-year-old might enjoy. When Casey had showed them a way to fold notebook paper into the shape of a bird that flapped its wings, Faith instantly made one to mail home to her little brother.

From little stories that Faith told about her mother, Dana felt that they had the same kind of warm, playful relationship that Dana enjoyed with her own mother.

When it came to Faith's father, everything changed. Dana had watched Faith from across the room the first time he was mentioned. Faith's lovely face seemed to harden. Her voice was strange, as if she were speaking something she had memorized without dwelling on the meaning of the words.

"Killed in the line of duty as a police officer," Faith said, quickly turning the talk to other things.

Dana understood this feeling. Even after all this time, she couldn't bring herself to say about her parents, "They're divorced," without it bringing a fresh slice of pain.

"Wouldn't you give anything to be able to hear up?" Faith whispered. "Like clear through the ceiling and Alison's rug?"

"We almost can," Dana replied. "Listen to that."

Sure enough, they heard the sound of hurried footsteps, which would have been inaudible in anything but perfect silence. Then there was the vibration of a door being closed firmly and the creaking of the wooden floor above.

Wordlessly, they both started for their own door, reaching it at the same moment. Faith cautioned Dana with an upraised hand before easing it open by a careful rotation of the knob. Muted safety lights gleamed from the ends of the hall as they stood in their open doorway to listen.

Faith had complained bitterly about those uncarpeted stairs when she was moving her things up the long flights to the fourth floor. "In my next childhood I am going to a school that knows about elevators," she had told anyone who would listen.

Suddenly those same uncarpeted stairs were their friends. Footsteps were coming swiftly from above. That had to be Alison. Her top floor apartment, known as the penthouse, was the only living area on that floor. But the footsteps didn't sound like Alison, who managed never to give any sense of haste or lack of control.

Now and then Alison's quick tread caught a creaky board and Faith winced at Dana's side. Cringing against their door in the darkness, they watched Alison cross the landing.

Alison, slender and really tall — almost six feet — always looked graceful and statuesque. There in that half-light she looked like something from a very dramatic play. Her wild shoulder-length hair glistened in the gleam of the muted lights at the turn of the stair. Her thick red robe was tied with a silken rope, whose tassles danced behind her. On anyone else, slippers without backs always flapped. Alison moved in them as gracefully as a dancer. Only the concerned look on her face betrayed that this was not an ordinary errand she was on.

Dana and Faith might have followed her down the stairs that moment if it hadn't been for the light. Dana barely suppressed a gasp as an arc of sudden light illuminated the room behind them, an almost blinding flash of light coming into the darkness.

As Dana whirled, the windows turned dark again. Faith moved swiftly to lean on her hands and stare down into the circle driveway in front of Baker House.

Faith whistled softly. "Now, will you look at that? Just like the White House or Embassy Row."

Faith's comparison was natural enough for a girl from the capital. Dana's own reaction had been that the scene reminded her of Park Avenue outside the Waldorf on a weekend, or maybe one of the Broadway theaters on an opening night.

The flash had come from headlights. Three cars, all long, all black, and all gleaming under the lanterns of the drive, had pulled to a stop and simultaneously hooded their lights. As if on a signal, uniformed men stepped from the first and last car. Only when they had quickly glanced around, did the driver of the middle car get out to walk briskly to the rear door.

The woman he helped out was small. Her face was hidden by their angle of view, but she was enveloped in pale fur and was wearing very high heels. The man who stepped out behind her and took her arm was tall and sturdily built. A great mass of snow-white hair glistened in the light.

"That must be who called Alison," Faith said. "Let's go." She tugged at Dana's sleeve.

"No, wait," Dana urged. "Maybe they have Shelley with them."

Faith, leaning her forehead against the cold pane of the window, cried out suddenly. "Dana, I know that man. I've seen his face before. But where?"

Even as she spoke, the couple disappeared from view as they entered Baker House.

"Casey's parents," Faith decided aloud. "At least, that's Casey's father. I recognize him from one of the pictures I have there in my closet. I took all the stuff Casey threw out and stashed it away for her."

Dana studied her friend. None of this was making any sense. Shelley was missing. Casey's parents, who had not planned to come to Parent-Alumnae Weekend at all, were showing up in the middle of the night when everything was all over.

"Now maybe Casey will get lucky and see what a fool she made of herself," Faith said quietly.

Dana looked at her friend thoughtfully. Casey had already gotten lucky when she acquired Faith for a friend. Everyone else had lost patience with Casey before the fall term even settled down. Casey had hit Canby Hall as if she were out to make the *Guinness Book of World Records* for broken rules. She acted as if having a problem gave her a license to make problems for everyone else, too.

Everybody has problems. There was simply no such thing as a person without a problem.

Dana herself admitted that she hadn't learned to handle her parents' divorce. She couldn't make herself accept the forever of it. Only her dream that someday they would all be a family again made her able to keep an uneasy grip on her emotions about it.

And look at Shelley. Instead of accepting Canby Hall as the great place it was, she had spent half the year mooning about some hick boyfriend she had left back home in Iowa.

But Casey had problems on top of her problems. Not only was she ridiculously daring about rules and behavior, but she spent her energy on helpless fury at her parents. If Faith hadn't played social worker and talked her out of running away earlier in the year, heaven knows where she would be. But this last blowup had definitely been a setback. Casey had seemed to be straightening out and settling down when that letter came from her parents, telling her that they couldn't make it to Greenleaf for Parent-Alumnae Weekend.

"Can't come," Casey had raged, throwing the letter across the room. "They can make it to Madrid and Paris and the ends of the world, but they can't come a little north of Boston for their own kid. I should have been born an oil painting. Then I would have been able to attract their attention." The upshot of that tantrum was that she cleaned out her room. She threw away every gift her parents had given her. She pitched out two whole shoeboxes full of letters from them and a framed picture of her father taken at some pier in Europe with a flag-draped liner in the background.

"Come on, let's go down," Dana urged as the three cars idled in the drive below them.

Dana and Faith made it down the first

flight of stairs easily enough. Faith had taught Dana and Shelley how to get down stairs without being heard. You hefted your weight onto the bannister and sort of slid down on the butts of your hands, barely touching the stairs with your feet.

From the last landing they saw that Alison had apparently taken the guests into the parlor. A thick line of yellow light fanned from under the door into the hall. Through the glass panels by the front windows they could see the dark glint of the limousines still waiting outside.

From the landing they could hear only the faintest rumble of sound from behind the closed parlor door.

Dana didn't so much whisper the question as breathe it. "Do we dare get any closer?"

Faith was deciding with a frown when the door suddenly swung open. Alison stood against the light a moment before coming out into the hall. The woman in the fur and the white-haired man followed her. As Alison extinguished the light in the room they had left, she flipped on the hall lights.

Only someone who knew her well would realize how hard Alison was straining to keep her voice calm.

"Obviously the first thing to do is check Casey's room. Please be careful on the stairs."

As she spoke, she and the others started for the stairway where Faith and Dana were crouching. Dana and Faith barely made it to an alcove at the top of the stairs before Alison and the Flints passed so near that a wave of Mrs. Flint's perfume seemed to envelop them.

"There's still a chance that this is all a bluff," Mr. Flint was assuring his wife in a careful whisper.

Casey's mother had more trouble concealing the tears behind her voice. "When I think of all the pains we have gone to, I can't believe this can happen. Sometimes it seemed to me that the police were going to extraordinary precautions — almost to the point of silliness. How could I have been so wrong?"

"Don't think like that," her husband said. They had moved farther down the hall. Dana had to strain to hear his whispered words. "Who would have thought they would think to kidnap our child?"

Dana felt her breath ease from her lungs painfully. She felt herself begin to shiver that miserable way you do when you are cold and past even believing in warmth again. Turning, she caught Faith close, clinging to her there in the darkness.

"Kidnap." Faith's voice registered astonishment. "But that's impossible."

Dana was still struggling to make her own breath come evenly.

"Really impossible," Faith assured her. "You see, Casey is here, right in her room where she is supposed to be. I tried to get her to talk to me when I was looking for Shelley. She wouldn't even answer me. She was just lying there on her stomach, pretending not to be crying. I finally shut the door and went away."

CHAPTER THREE

By using the other stairwell, Dana and Faith could reach Casey's floor without being close enough to risk being seen by her parents and Alison. By the time they reached the top of the stairs, Alison was moving down the hall toward Casey's door.

"Casey's there," Faith repeated in a careful whisper. "She really is in there."

Dana nodded in the darkness. It wasn't that she didn't believe Faith, it just seemed terribly confusing that Mr. and Mrs. Flint would come in that impressive caravan unless they had some good reason to believe Casey was missing.

"Alison's alone there at Casey's door," Faith said with astonishment. "Where are Casey's parents?"

"Maybe they're waiting," Dana guessed. "Alison will probably try not to startle Casey too much."

24

Alison didn't even rap at Casey's door. She just disappeared into Casey's room. After what seemed a very long time, she returned with Casey following. Casey was bundled in the familiar tartan plaid robe that she had worn to breakfast her first week (against the rules, of course).

Casey wasn't even listening to Alison, who was trying to get her to keep her voice low. Instead, in typical Casey fashion, she was arguing defensively as she tried to pull away from Alison. Her hair was a mass of rumpled blond curls, and her voice was thickened from sleep and tears.

"I didn't do anything," Casey was protesting. "What's all this about? Let go of me."

Alison's reply was a murmur that Dana didn't catch. Casey's response was swift and violent. She shoved Alison aside. Grabbing her robe tighter, she would have fled back into the room if Alison had not been holding her arm.

"No," Casey was insisting angrily. "Let me go. Just let me go."

"But your mother and father . . ." Alison was saying.

Casey was clearly losing the battle against fresh tears. But even with her voice tremulous, her words were harsh and cold. "Don't even talk to me about them. I'm just as interested in them as they are in me. Now let me go."

At Faith's faint gasp, Dana followed her glance. The dim glow of the security lights on the stairs revealed Mr. and Mrs. Flint huddled there hearing their daughter's angry words.

"Let go of me," Casey was threatening. "Let go or I'll scream." Although Alison was tall, this would have been an equal contest. Casey, although small, was a coiled spring of fury who would resort to fighting in ways that Alison would never think of.

Casey's father stepped up to the hall level first. Even that dim, hooded security light at the landing was enough to light up that spectacular head of white hair. His face was in darkness, preventing Dana from seeing his expression, but he spoke his daughter's name in a stricken tone.

"Casey," he said.

At her name, Casey whirled. She stared at him an endless moment before moving. Dana felt that sudden shiver of pain that came when *her* mother and father exchanged furious, hurting words.

"Oh, please don't blow it," she was whispering to herself. "Just this once, Casey, don't blow it."

She needn't have been afraid. With a little moan that sounded wounded, Casey flew across the hall to land against her father's chest. "Daddy," she cried with disbelief. Then as she looked past him, "And Mom. Oh . . . oh."

All in a rush they were in each other's arms. Casey was tight against her mother's shoulder as her father's arms caught both of them in a giant hug. Casey's mother kept repeating, "My baby. My baby," in a croon that was a half-sob.

"But why? How?" Casey asked. "I don't understand. You said . . ."

"I know what we said." Her father's tone was patient. "But . . ."

"How about coming up to my place?" Alison asked in a careful whisper.

"Ah, yes," Mr. Flint said, glancing down the hall as if just remembering where they were. Dana felt her heart slam against her ribs as his eyes swept the stairs where she and Faith were crouching in the dark.

As Casey and her parents disappeared up the stairs with Alison, Casey still clung to them both. Only when they were gone from sight did Dana realize that Faith, at her side, didn't even seem to be breathing.

"Faith," Dana said softly. "Hey there."

In answer Faith slid to the floor to sit with her knees up tight against her chest. Her head was bent, and she rocked a little there in the shadows.

Dana had felt a wave of painful homesickness at this touching reunion between Casey and her parents. But even knowing that such a scene was unlikely for her ever again, it couldn't have hurt her like it must have Faith.

More than anything, Dana wanted to kneel

beside Faith and hold her tightly. Even when she was on her knees beside her friend, something held her back. Over and over in the months they had been friends, Dana had seen Faith exert an unbelievable strength against adversity. Maybe this same strength kept Dana from reaching out. It was as if Faith were wordlessly telling her that she would handle her problems alone.

Dana, feeling Faith's pain as her own, waited — thinking, as she had many times before, that Faith's father must have been an extraordinary man.

Dana knew little about him except that he had been killed in the line of duty as a police officer. What Dana did know was that the pain of that loss was undiminished by time. Faith's voice, ordinarily bright and crisp, changed to something flowing and melodious when she spoke his name. It was as if the very memory of his gentleness softened her, making her suddenly vulnerable.

Dana, waiting there in the dark, fought a sudden rush of hot tears at her own helplessness.

Then Faith, with a swift shake of her head, as if to free herself of something unseen, raised her head and grinned at Dana ruefully.

With a smooth grace she swung her arms and rose to her feet, tightening her robe belt with a swift gesture.

"Well," Faith said softly. "That was a three-tissue scenario if I ever saw one. What kind of nut went out of his way to scare a nice family like that? Whoever made that crank call is my candidate for the creep of the year."

Dana didn't have the energy to reel off the floor like Faith had. She only sat there, feeling the icy surface of the wooden planks through her pajamas and robe as she stared into the darkness.

"Something wrong?" Faith asked, leaning down to her.

"Maybe they didn't know it was a lie," Dana suggested, not meaning for her voice to sound so tiny and hesitant.

Faith knelt by her. "Now, come on, Dana. You saw Casey yourself this time. You know the call had to be some practical joker."

Dana shook her head. Something hard and painful was knotting itself in her throat, making it hard to talk. But she had to say it, no matter how much she hated to.

"Maybe they really thought they did have Casey," she told Faith. "After all, a girl is missing . . . Shelley."

Faith was now all the way back down on the floor by Dana, gripping her arm as if to bring her to her senses.

"That's crazy and you know it, Dana Morrison. Why would anyone want to kidnap Shelley?"

"Why would anyone want to kidnap

Casey?" Dana countered. "But take the case that somebody did and got the wrong girl just by mistake?"

"Mistake," Faith hooted. "Come on, Dana. Shelley and Casey aren't exactly peas in a pod, you know. Only a real fool could take one of them for the other."

"A fool or a stranger," Dana insisted. "Think a minute. You know how much Casey has changed since you got her going to that counselor."

"Okay, okay," Faith conceded a little crossly. "So Casey has changed and all for the better. But she didn't change enough that she and Shelley are a matched set. Nobody snatches a banana thinking it is an apple."

"No more wild tricks," Dana reminded her. "No more insane tantrums. Not even a raised voice until that thing about Parent-Alumnae Weekend came up. You said yourself that Casey was a new girl."

"But not Shelley!" Faith countered.

"The hair," Dana reminded her. "The clothes . . ."

Faith groaned, making it unnecessary for Dana to finish the recital. The close-cropped hair that Casey wore had grown and been curled over the Christmas holidays. The style and length were just like Shelley's.

Faith's dark eyes were luminous in that dimness. "The clothes," she repeated numbly. "Even the clothes . . ."

Shelley had returned after Christmas with three new sweaters and a white, quilted down parka. Within a week Casey had abandoned her usual uniform of oversized sweat shirts and had bought a bunch of sweaters and a parka that was a twin to Shelley's.

"She's only trying to make herself over into the same neat kind of person that you are," Faith had told Shelley. "When you aren't satisfied with yourself, you look around for someone you wish you could be like. It's the same thing that has half the kids in this dorm on diets or fooling with their hair color." Then Faith had grinned at her. "Come on, Shelley, haven't you ever been guilty of copying someone you admired?"

Dana could almost see Shelley's anger change to amused remembrance. Then Shelley grinned, too.

"I was a lot younger than Casey," she said. "Her name was — and still is — Angela. I spent two years trying to make myself over into Angela. She won a prize for bread at the state fair when she was in the fourth grade. I took up cooking. She was the best swimmer at the park pool in the sixth grade. I bullied my brothers into coaching me in swimming. I finally figured out that a real Shelley was better than an imitation Angela and I was just copycatting."

Dana had chuckled. "If anyone cares, the girl *I* copycatted was named Lori. Among other things, she had a delicious German accent. My family nearly destroyed themselves with hysterical laughter at my trying that, then I finally gave up."

"I hate to repeat clichés," Faith said. "But imitation is still the sincerest form of flattery."

"I wish she couldn't afford to be so sincere," Shelley said, the anger all gone. "She can afford to change her wardrobe with the drop of a credit card. I'm hung with mine. I must admit, though, that she looks better since she's traded in those awful cowboy boots for nice trim loafers like mine."

"Give her time," Faith said. "She's just trying to find herself."

"I'm just sorry she has to crawl through my wardrobe in her search," Shelley said. Then after a glance at Faith, she had shrugged. "She can have all the time she needs, I guess. Maybe I'll even get used to feeling like one of those paper dolls that you cut out from folded notebook paper."

Faith had laughed. "Just be thankful that the green lines don't show."

Dana was not so much suggesting added evidence for her theory as thinking aloud. "Then there was Casey's Aunt Edie from Boston. It was Shelley that met her at the train, had breakfast with her, and then brought her out here to the campus. It was Shelley who took her around, introducing her to everyone but the statue of the lioness out by the wishing pond."

"Did she actually see Casey's aunt to the train when she left?" Faith asked.

Dana nodded. "I think she did. It would be like Shelley to play hostess to the last good-bye."

"That does it," Faith said, springing to her feet with a new urgency in her voice. "Only a stranger could have mistaken them, but a stranger would be up to no good at all. We've got to talk to Alison."

Then, after tugging Dana to her feet, she paused. "Casey's folks should be leaving soon. After all, it's almost Monday morning by now."

Glancing at her watch, Dana realized that it had been almost eighteen hours since she had seen Shelley. "We can't wait for them to leave," she told Faith. "We've waited too long already."

Mounting the stairs to the floor where Alison had her apartment wasn't too difficult. But outside Alison's door Faith and Dana began a silent head-shaking argument about who would knock.

Dana lost. When she lifted her hand to rap at the door, she found herself suddenly trembling again.

The sounds from inside were muffled, the rise and fall of Casey's voice against the rumble of her father's deeper tones. Alison had to be serving something. Dana heard the faint clink of something like a spoon against china and the conversational mewing of Alison's cat, Doby. She even imagined a faintly almond smell to the air outside the door.

With an exasperated shrug, Faith took Dana's hand and rapped on the door panel softly.

Alison swung the door open during a sudden silence. The light was blinding as Doby switched past his mistress to rub himself companionably against Dana's leg.

Dana had loved Alison's apartment from the first time she had been there. But suddenly the posters that dominated the wall seemed too bright. The old neon sign from KATIE'S KLIP AND KURL seemed garish in the light of her fear. Mr. and Mrs. Flint sat in two armchairs behind the coffee table. Casey, puzzled, was between them on a pillow on the floor.

The nearly demolished plate of coffee cake on the table explained the scent of almonds. The cluster of bright mugs here and there suggested the happiest kind of tea party.

"Faith," Alison was saying, her voice as puzzled as Casey's face. "Dana . . . what in the world?"

Dana thought she had memorized the words. She was going to come to the point, in the politest kind of way. Instead she found herself stammering. "We have to. I'm sorry."

In the end it was Faith who reached out a slender hand to touch Alison's arm.

"We're awfully sorry," she said carefully, "but we had to tell you that we can't find Shelley anywhere. She's gone — simply gone."

CHAPTER FOUR

From the door of Alison's room Dana had a clear view of Casey Flint. She was between her parents, basking in the warm glow of Alison's lamp. Casey had never looked so pretty. Even with her hair tousled from sleep, she looked beautiful, her face glowing with happiness.

For one second all of them registered Faith's words in silence. Then, to Dana's astonishment, Casey exploded into laughter. The sound froze Dana. She was too amazed even to feel angry. Dana stared at her in disbelief as the sound hung in that frozen air.

Maybe Dana would have liked Mr. Flint no matter what conditions she met him under. But he certainly won her heart in that split second. Even as he put a firm, restraining hand on his daughter's knee, he rose to his feet. He seemed like a giant in that room, scarcely clearing the primitive overhead pipes that Alison had livened with brilliantly colored paint. His eyes were darker than Casey's beneath astonishingly dark brows. His face was deeply tanned and seamed with smile lines.

But now he wasn't smiling.

"Gone," he repeated, studying Dana's and Faith's faces. "What do you mean . . . gone?"

Casey tugged at his jacket. "Daddy, they have to be kidding. Shelley's not the wild sort. She'd never think of running away. This is some kind of joke."

Mr. Flint didn't seem to hear his daughter. He was at the door beside Alison in a few purposeful steps.

"Is this true?" he asked Alison. "Is there a girl missing?"

Suddenly it was Alison who was stammering. "I don't know," she said, looking first at Dana and then at Faith. "This is the very first I have heard of this. Surely if someone had been missing at bed check, I would have been notified."

When neither Dana nor Faith responded, Alison's voice rose. "What about the monitor? Surely . . ."

Dana felt herself flush with resentment. Didn't Alison realize that reporting on a monitor was the same as tattling? It wasn't that she didn't like Heather Blackburn, but the monitor was not among her closest friends. And as for going to Heather with anything, that was out of the question. Heather was a hopeless worrier who blew every tiny thing up into a federal case.

"I think Heather went to bed a little early," Faith said, meeting Alison's eyes very directly.

"We missed Shelley at ten-thirty," Dana said. "At first we thought maybe she had been delayed in getting back from town."

"Town?" Alison asked.

"She was seeing a guest off on the train," Faith filled in.

Casey's laughter had stilled. Her eyes darkened as she watched and listened. Dana felt her trying to catch her eyes, but the memory of that laughter still rang in Dana's ears. She avoided Casey's glance.

"Ten-thirty," Alison said, her voice rising a little. "And you still haven't located her?"

Mrs. Casey, slender in a knitted sheath, had joined her husband at the door. Their obvious concern was evident as she slid her arm through his and leaned a little against him as if for support.

"Is it possible that your friend didn't get back from town?"

"The monitor —" Alison began, then broke off. "That should be easy enough to check from the sign-in sheet down in the hall." But even as she turned, her look at Dana was one of reproach. "I can't imagine that you let this go on so long."

"We were on our way up here to tell you when . . ." Dana's voice trailed off as she met Mr. Flint's eyes.

"When the cars came up and people came in. We waited to see if it might be something about Shelley," Faith explained.

Mr. Flint frowned as he studied them, but his voice was gentle. "Then you must know why we came."

Faith nodded. "We heard," she admitted.

"I'll go check," Alison said, letting herself out the door. From the sharp staccato sound from the stairs, Dana knew that Alison was running all the way down to the door of their room, where their sign-in sheet was posted.

Casey, still among the pillows, stared from one to the other with a stormy expression. She started to her feet only to catch her heel in her robe hem and tumble back again. "What's going on here?" she asked in that old belligerent tone. "What's all this stuff, any-way?"

"Wait a bit," her mother coaxed.

The cat Doby had shot out of the door ahead of his mistress. He returned the same way, skittering into the door and leaping onto a pillow when Alison opened the door to come back in. It was clear that she didn't bear good news. She closed the door quietly and leaned against it. The color was gone from her face, and she closed her eyes a brief moment as if catching her sight as well as her breath.

"Shelley isn't signed in," she said at last. "She signed out to see a visitor to the train. The sheet said she should have returned before ten. There is no signature on the sign-in line."

Mr. Flint turned away from the doorway and started for the phone by the kitchen door. With his hand on it, he paused.

"Now, have you girls really looked for her? She didn't just decide to spend the night in a friend's room?"

"We looked everywhere we could possibly think of," Faith replied. "I don't think she's anywhere in Baker House."

"Faith," Casey wailed. "Dana, what's going on? Can't somebody tell me what this is all about?"

Her father turned and caught her in the curve of his free arm and rubbed his cheek against her head. "Hang on a minute, love. You'll get the whole story. But first things first."

Later Dana was astonished to remember how swiftly Mr. Flint was able to get in touch with the FBI without even checking for a number. By then she knew that Casey's father had talked to the federal authorities earlier. Because he was involved in a federal trial, the usual twenty-four hour delay for the FBI to enter a kidnap case was not observed. At that moment Dana was only impressed by his clear tone of authority in dealing with the voice at the other end of the phone.

"Jason Flint here," he said. "There has been a kidnap warning and a girl is missing from Canby Hall, just out from Greenleaf. It is crucial that you arrive without exciting any attention. You will find security guards waiting in the circle drive in front of Baker House. You will need to identify yourselves to them. How soon can we expect you?" After a moment of silence, he replaced the phone.

Alison had made her way to a chair near the door and let herself down into it as if she had suddenly learned that she was breakable.

Casey, in the curve of her father's arm, was wide-eyed and speechless. He led her to the cushions and pulled her down beside him. "We haven't met," he said to Faith and Dana, "but which one of you is volunteering to put on fresh water for tea?"

Dana moved carefully in the kitchenette so as not to miss a word from the next room. When the water began to rumble in Alison's copper pot, Dana searched through candy jars until she located a cache of tea leaves. As the tea steeped she braced herself in the door, trying to stop the trembling that had begun when she and Faith had knocked on Alison's door.

"Let me begin at the beginning, Casey," he said. "You know that your mother and I spend a lot of time abroad finding things for Flint Gallery. We buy collection pieces for our clients, works by new artists, and things for museums."

"I know all that," Casey interrupted. "What has it got to do with Shelley?"

"Stay with me," he told her. "Many of our clients are partial to certain schools of art. They may buy some minor pieces by a new artist but will often want a good copy of a well-known artist's work to hang in an exhibition room. About a year ago we ran across the work of a man in Europe who makes such magnificent copies that even your mother, who is famous for her skill, was almost fooled."

"Fakes?" Casey asked in disbelief. "You buy fakes?"

"Only for people who want them," he explained. "In the last year we have imported six works by this copyist. Three of them have been stolen from the gallery."

Casey nodded. "I remember the first break-in."

"There was a second one, and only copies were stolen again. It was kind of a joke for a while. Then last fall, on our trip to Europe, we had time for some museum prowling. We were looking at the originals of the pictures that we had ordered copied. Your mother created a scene, claiming the museum had a copy. At first the director was insulted, but upon examination she proved to be right."

"You mean you were selling a copy of a copy?" Casey asked.

He shook his head. "It was worse than that. This was a giant swindle. The criminals were using us to achieve their ends. After we examined and accepted the copies, the criminal replaced them with stolen originals. So the pictures we imported to America were originals, but we didn't know it. Then, one by one, they were stealing back from us the originals, which we unknowingly had to sell. The copies were hung in European museums in the place of the stolen originals."

"What a rotten deal," Casey exploded.

"You might say that, but more than that, we felt responsible. We have been working with the government ever since, doing all we can to help them build a strong case against the thieves. Now our testimony is vital to the government case because the originals stolen from us have never been found."

Alison, rising to pass a cup of tea to Mrs. Flint, paused and walked to the window.

"The FBI must be here," she told Mr. Flint quietly. "At least, a new car is coming up the drive."

As Mr. Flint left with Alison to go downstairs, Casey turned to her mother.

"Then you're in danger?" she asked quietly. "That's why you left during Christmas when I was home? That's why you didn't come this weekend?"

Her mother nodded and tightened her lips. "Honey, we had no choice. There was too much at risk."

"Explain that," Casey said.

Her mother dropped her eyes. "There were two attempts on your father's life and mine before we really believed that we needed to go into hiding and stay under guard."

Casey grabbed her mother and hugged her so tightly that Dana wondered how Mrs. Flint could breathe. Then Casey drew back and stared at her mother.

Her mother took Casey's hand. "A little before midnight we got a call telling us that they had kidnapped you and would hold you until after the trial to insure that we wouldn't testify against the criminal."

"They were lying," Casey said flatly. "Just a big, giant lie to scare you into not testifying." At her mother's sober expression she paused, confused. "But Shelley? What good would it do if they kidnapped Shelley? That would be stupid."

Glancing at Faith, Dana saw her friend's face carefully empty of expression. No one said a word. No one reminded Casey that she had spent the past few weeks becoming a carbon copy of Shelley. Maybe someone should have. When Casey thought it through for herself, the idea hit her with a painful impact. Her face was suddenly stripped of color, and she clung to her mother.

"*No,*" she said firmly. "*No.* They wouldn't have mistaken Shelley for me. What have I done?" she whispered almost to herself. "Maybe they did think Shelley was me."

Dana had never seen Casey really cry. She had seen her yell and storm and use words that would have earned her permanent detention if Alison had overheard them, but she had never seen her cry. The tears simply fell. Casey didn't even lift a hand to her face. Her slow sobbing even hurt to listen to. "My fault," she said dully. "I was so selfish that I put Shelley in danger. What will they do when they find out they have the wrong girl? They won't hurt her, will they?"

Dana looked up to meet Faith's eyes. Faith looked away. They hadn't gotten that far in their thinking.

What would the kidnappers do when they discovered they had a girl who didn't matter to them at all?

There were steps outside the door. Mr. Flint entered, followed by two trim young men whose eyes seemed to absorb everything in the room in a single glance.

When swift introductions had been made, Alison asked, "Would you prefer that Faith and Dana return to their rooms?"

The older of the two men studied Dana's face soberly for a moment and then Faith's. "Mr. Flint had very little chance to brief us on the way upstairs. However, from what he said, I feel that not only are all of us in this together, but that these two young ladies may be of immense help to us."

He paused and frowned a little to himself.

"How old are you?" he asked Faith suddenly.

"Fifteen," she replied. "All of us are."

"Fifteen," he echoed. "I hate to see you caught in an affair like this, but it's too late for regrets. But what I must tell you at once is that kidnapping, like any act of terrorism involving hostages, is a dangerous and unpredictable thing. The life of your friend may depend on our handling this with delicacy and discretion. A single slip of the tongue could have fatal consequences."

Dana felt his words hit her almost physically. Hostage. Fatal consequences. She couldn't have said a word to save her life. She only nodded, holding her breath.

Faith's voice came low and gentle. "We understand," she said. "You can depend on us."

Casey had slumped back onto the pillows with her head in her hands, weeping softly. She didn't even seem to notice her mother trying to draw her close. "What have I done?" she kept whispering. "What have I done?"

CHAPTER FIVE

Shelley Hyde faced Parent-Alumnae week-end with very mixed emotions. More than anything, she wanted her own parents there, along with her great brothers. Not only would she have loved to show them off to her friends, but she wanted to share Canby Hall with them. They had all pored over the pictures when she was considering the school the summer before. They knew what the campus looked like. Jeff had even whistled as he studied the picture of Main Building, with its fine old bell tower and the graceful brick fronts of the dormitories.

"It doesn't even look like America," he said. "It looks like the setting of a fancy English movie."

"And look at those stables!" her brother Larry had added.

At that time Shelley had been less than interested. She had wanted to stay in Pine

Bluff at her same old high school, meeting Paul for sodas after school and having him hold her hand through whatever movie finally made its way to the Orpheum in Pine Bluff. Filled with resentment, she had felt that this "great opportunity" of going to Canby Hall was only a way for her parents to keep her away from Paul. But the same months that had brought her so close to Faith and Dana had turned Canby Hall into her own world. More than anything she wanted her family to see the place as she did.

Naturally that was out of the question. Both of her brothers were in school at Iowa State University in Ames and could hardly get the time, even if they could afford the trip to Massachusetts.

Her father had a living to make in his hardware store. Weekend trips to Massachusetts were out of the question for an ordinary family with two sons in college and a daughter in boarding school.

As it turned out, not having her own parents there was not the worst of the weekend at all. The worst was that Shelley had gotten herself involved with a woman she had never met and was faced with two whole days of trying to make her happy.

It was all Casey Flint's fault for being such a baby. But if Shelley had been able to keep her mouth shut, she wouldn't have offered to take over Casey's aunt from Boston.

But she hadn't kept her mouth shut. Now she was in for it.

Since the Christmas break, Casey had gotten on her nerves more than she let even Dana and Faith know. Every time Shelley picked up a fork in the dining room, Casey was watching so she could pick up hers the same way. Casey had her hair styled like Shelley's and bleached a little to match the color. In truth, Shelley wasn't sure about the bleaching, but Casey's hair had certainly looked darker when it was cropped close to her head.

Casey had thrown such a super fit when she heard that her own mother and dad weren't coming that Shelley had been disgusted. She was acting like a half-grown kid. Back in Pine Bluff when Shelley had done a lot of baby-sitting, she had often been able to shame a ten-year-old into doing something by offering to do it herself.

Her attempt to shame Casey into being civil to her aunt had backfired.

"All right, Miss Goody Two Shoes," Casey had flared. "Her name is Edith Flint, and she'll be staying at the Inn in town. You might want to take earplugs — she never shuts up." Casey had started out the door, only to slam back, glaring at Shelley. "And she never goes home, either. You can figure on being stuck with her until the late train on Sunday night."

On Friday night Shelley had sat by the phone a long time before getting up the nerve to call the Inn and ask for Casey's aunt.

The girls at Canby Hall decided that the telephone system at the Inn had been installed for the use of the patriots during the Revolutionary War and that the plumbing had gone in the same week. When the clerk finally got Edith Flint on the phone, Shelley was pleasantly surprised by the brightness in the older woman's voice. It was easier than she had feared to explain that she would be Aunt Edith's hostess for the weekend.

"What a nice thing to do," Casey's aunt said, then paused, the faint singing of the bad connection almost overpowering her words. "I hope nothing's wrong with Casey."

Nothing that a good swat on the tail wouldn't cure, Shelley thought to herself. "It's more that she has committed herself to other things," Shelley said. That was true enough. Casey had pledged to be an absolute brat and meant to go through with it.

"Ten o'clock tomorrow?" the voice went on. "And call me Aunt Edie; almost everyone does. But what about breakfast? I'd love to have you be my guest here at the Inn. That way we could get acquainted before we start our day."

Aunt Edie had inadvertently hit Shelley's weak point. Breakfast at Canby Hall was enough to ruin your day. Breakfast at the Inn meant hot blueberry muffins and mounds of fluffy scrambled eggs ringed with crisp bacon.

"That's awfully nice of you." Shelley hesitated.

"It would be nice of *you*," Aunt Edie insisted. "I simply can't wait to meet you, and I find eating alone is boring."

"Good," she said briskly when Shelley agreed. "I'll be waiting in the breakfast room about eight-thirty. Do take a cab and let me pay for it."

Shelley had declined the cab. The brisk walk through the woods to the village would make her feel less guilty about the extra calories she knew she would get at breakfast. As she unwound her muffler at the door, the rich smell of coffee and the tang of bacon overpowered her. She hoped that Casey's breakfast toast was just as anemic and tooth-resistant as usual.

The breakfast room at the Inn looked almost like a sun porch, with small-paned windows bright along the walls. Big pots of Swedish ivy and fern hung along the sunny walls. The tables were set with yellow stoneware with a single bayberry candle on each to match the deep tones of the flowered yellow-and-green napkins. All was not lost. Parent-Alumnae Weekend was clearly looking up.

The woman who rose as Shelley entered brought an instant chuckle to Shelley's throat. Edith Flint was extremely tall and bone-slender with graying hair drawn back in a soft, low bun at the nape of her neck. She wore light makeup and the eyes behind her glasses glowed with warmth. Shelley felt as if she had known her forever. She could imagine her at her father's hardware store or in Boston, fingering gloves at Filene's. Shelley's quick hug and the kiss on her cheek astonished Aunt Edie right back into her seat.

The blueberry muffins were so hot that they simply breathed in the wedges of butter. There was also cranberry walnut bread in a small, fat loaf that Aunt Edie sliced briskly and layered with butter for Shelley.

Aunt Edie was wonderfully easy to talk to. One simply gave her a phrase and she galloped off with it, recounting every one she had ever known from Iowa. How marvelous it would be to have older brothers as Shelley had; her own brother, Jason, Casey's father, was younger, but still a simply marvelous person.

"Casey is all right, isn't she?" she asked quietly after a few minutes. Her eyes were intent on Shelley's face. "I know she must have been upset about her parents not coming."

"She was upset," Shelley admitted. "She still is. Sometimes it's hard for her to understand why they don't get to see her more often."

Aunt Edie shook her head. "It's impossible to understand even when you're a thousand years old like I am."

Suddenly she launched into the first of the peculiar conversations that kept swimming to the surface during their next two days together.

"It all started with that *Madonna of the Roses,*" she said crossly. "Not that it isn't a magnificent picture. Have you seen it, dear?"

At Shelley's confused shake of her head, Aunt Edie leaned forward.

"It's not your run-of-the-gallery Madonna, you see. Not that I am against those. The mother is not really a woman, she's more like a very young girl. Confused, you know, with her lovely heart-shaped face still glowing from childhood. She's leaning over the child, and her dark curls are wreathed with scarlet roses. You can't see the baby in her lap. It's hidden by folds of a shawl, but all the light in the picture is coming from that unseen child. It lights the girl's face and touches the petals of the roses with a curious luminous glow. But it's been such a terrible thing, having it stolen and all."

Then seeing the confusion in Shelley's face, she laughed. "There I go, on and on. You did know that Casey's parents have this wonderful art gallery? I never miss a new painting they get in. That one was so unforgettable that I went straight to it every time

I was there. Then it had to be stolen in the robbery. But enough of that. Are you sure we shouldn't send for more muffins?"

Shelley groaned. "If I eat another bite I'll have to go sleep it off. We have too full a day planned for that."

The day was as much fun as it was busy. Aunt Edie's low-heeled shoes carried her relentlessly from event to event. She especially enjoyed the display in the art department, standing a long time before the better paintings, stepping back with a little squint to see them from a better angle.

"Casey's talented," she nodded. "But something is standing between her and her brush. I hope it isn't jealousy of her parents' time."

It was fun to introduce Aunt Edie to everyone on the staff and show her the special places on campus — the wooded walk, the grove of trees in a sort of magic circle, the stump of an oak that was said to have been there when Massachusetts was still a British colony.

Shelley went to bed Saturday night exhausted. Yet as she left Sunday for her breakfast date at the Inn with Aunt Edie, she realized that she was looking forward to another day with that doll. Before Shelley realized it, the weekend was over, and she and Aunt Edie were having their last meal together at the Inn. Aunt Edie's suitcase was waiting at the desk.

Shelley chose chicken pot pie because it sounded small. Aunt Edie laughed aloud when the steaming casserole was served.

"Not a little something from the supermarket you stick in an oven, is it?"

Nor did it taste like a frozen pie. Never had Shelley thought that she would rather keep eating that marvelous main course than go on to the Indian pudding with a dollop of cream, but she did.

"I can't tell you when I've had a better time," she told Aunt Edie sincerely as the waitress brought the check. "I've loved every single minute of it. Thank you for giving me an aunt for a weekend."

The eyes behind the glasses were suddenly misted. "So have I, Shelley. And I am the one who is thankful. Oh, I only wish I had something nice for you to remember our good time. I almost forgot what I brought for Casey." She dug in her purse and found a small brown envelope with the tab glued down. "I meant to wrap this for her, but the engraver only got it finished at the last minute. Would you mind taking it to Casey with my love? It's just a little bracelet that belonged to her grandmother, but time makes things precious to older people. I added her name on the inside to make it more personal."

With the envelope safe in her pocket, Shelley rushed Aunt Edie to the train station just as the last train was loading to depart. Shelley stood a long minute waving to her, a moving blue form behind the clouded window, until the train pulled out.

Casey was the loser, Shelley decided as she made her way out of the station. Poor Casey. Aunt Edie's chatter still filled Shelley's head, marvelous stories of artists and their friends, comments on paintings — particularly the *Madonna of the Roses* — and touching stories of Casey's childhood. It was pitiful that a girl who was loved so dearly could be so rotten to her family.

The train station had nearly emptied with the departure of the last train. Shelley was out of the door and into the lot outside before she realized that the taxi line was on the other side. As she turned to go back toward the cab station, a burly man lounging near the door called out to her.

"Over here, miss."

As she hesitated, she heard the motor of a van rumble as it drew alongside. Something prickled along the back of her neck, and she turned back toward the station door as fast as she could. She was too slow. His arm shot out and caught her, spinning her about and catching her with a leather-gloved hand tight across her face. She kicked frantically as he opened the back of the van and threw her inside. By the time he had bound her arms behind her back, the van was out on the street. Helplessly she saw the flash of street lights passing above her beyond the window.

She tried to scream and fight the rope on her hands, but it was useless. For his size, the man was agile. He crawled over the seat and took a place by the driver, looping his arm along the back to look back at her.

"So far so good," he said quietly to the driver. "She's a prickly little package."

"Runs in the family," the driver replied, making a sharp turn that threw Shelley painfully against the door handle of the van.

Exhausted from wrestling and pained from the scraping of the rope on her wrists, Shelley finally fell silent. She fought against tears: hopeless tears of frustration and fear.

They seemed to be driving forever, first smooth roads through a city or town, then the rougher roads of the countryside, the flashes of street lights gone. Once in a while her captors mumbled to themselves in tones too low for the words to be made out. Once the van stopped and the driver left for a few brief minutes. Her captor stared at her steadily until the van heaved a little from the weight of the driver getting back into the seat.

"Get him?" she heard him ask.

"His recorder," the man grumbled. "Just as good."

"Does he think he can be bumped off over a phone line?" The driver chuckled.

"He better be scared, especially now."

Shelley remembered a dozen stories she had read in which bound victims had wrestled loose to escape. Her tentative struggles only seemed to tighten the ropes around her wrists. Then she remembered the door handle she had fallen against. Slowly, an inch at a time, she wormed her way toward the door.

Her captor, glancing back, caught her in motion. "Okay, what do you think you're up to?"

"I'm stiff," she complained, "just moving around."

He watched her for a long time, during which she just flexed this muscle or that to convince him. Then, as the road turned really rough and he gave his attention to his companion's driving, Shelley felt her hand close over the door handle. She jerked it with all her strength. The door swung open, and she hurled herself into the darkness — hearing muttered curses and the screech of brakes as she fell.

CHAPTER SIX

Every morning at seven, Shelley's digital electric clock alarm went off with a steady, monotonous hum. Every morning without fail, Shelley's arm would emerge from under the comforter, grope for the clock, and knock off something. A book, a pencil, sometimes a bottle of nail polish would tumble off before she located the clock and silenced the alarm. At first Dana had thought Shelley was just plain awkward. In time she had learned better. Shelley had perfected the art of not opening her eyes, even a little, until she was standing in the shower. As weird as this was, Dana had soon realized that living with Shelley made mornings pretty entertaining. It was worth getting yourself wide awake to watch Shelley, her face blank from sleep, grope for a towel and soap and feel her way along the hall to the showers. One notable morning, Shelley had misjudged the distance and banged on the locked cleaning closet for several minutes before she and Faith went out to lead her to the proper door.

That Monday morning after Shelley's disappearance the alarm went off as usual. Dana and Faith, both exhausted from only a few hours of troubled sleep, heard it and groaned. Only when the sound continued did the horror of the night return to them.

Faith was out of bed and across the room in a flash to where they had put Shelley's clock. She started for the alarm, hesitated, then stopped to solemnly punch Shelley's pillow before silencing the alarm.

"Take that," she said in a funny, choked voice. Then slumping on Shelley's bed, she groaned. "This can't go on. It absolutely can't go on."

Dana wriggled up to a sitting position, holding her comforter tight around her chilled shoulders.

"You're right. It can't go on," she echoed numbly.

"And it's snowing," Faith added heavily.

Dana twisted to see out the windows. The flakes were coming down gently, drifting like minute scraps of paper. There was so little wind that you could follow the same flake of snow from the top of the high window, past the row of faceted crystals, down to the ledge that held their little collection of plants.

"What is today?" Faith asked after a moment.

"Monday," Dana decided aloud. "Monday the twenty-second of February."

"And when is that trial scheduled? The trial of the thieves that Mr. Flint has to testify against?"

"March first."

Faith went to her desk to lean over the calendar. "But that's eight whole days, Dana."

"Eight whole days," Dana repeated. It sounded like forever.

"There's an echo in here," Faith said, pulling her robe around her. At the door she paused. "What did Alison tell us last night?"

"Not to leave our rooms or go to breakfast until she talked with us," Dana reminded her.

"Did she tell us why?" Faith asked. "My head doesn't seem to be working very well."

"I gathered there would be some sort of plot hatched to conceal Shelley's disappearance."

"I don't want Shelley's disappearance hidden, I want it ended," Faith said hotly.

"But safely for Shelley," Dana reminded her.

"Safely for Shelley." Faith nodded. Then she grinned. "Like I said, there's an echo in here."

Faith and Dana waited, listening to the

usual early-morning clamor in the hall outside. Slippers slapped walking to the showers, someone shouted about missing a green sweater and got an equally loud denial. Only when the hall outside had quieted down did Dana hear a rattle like uneven wheels on the hall floor. Then a quick rap sounded at the door.

Alison had abandoned the woolly red robe for a trim cashmere sweater and pleated skirt, but the brightness of her lipstick was unconvincing.

"Hi," she said when Faith opened the door. "Give me a hand here."

The cart she pushed in was from the infirmary. A fresh towel concealed its contents from curious eyes.

"You must have attracted some attention coming down the hall with that," Faith observed, helping Alison get it over Shelley's braided rug.

Alison nodded. "I didn't mind. It clearly helped explain the quarantine sign I hung on your door last night."

"Quarantine sign!" Dana cried. "That's why we haven't had our usual parade of borrowers."

"They've been replaced by whispers," Alison said. She lifted the towel from the cart with a flourish. "Look what I brought."

She had not only raided the cafeteria but also her own apartment. There were cartons of milk and orange juice, a bowl filled with butter pats, a jar of raspberry jam (Alison's own), and a toaster for the stack of whole wheat bread.

"Genuine toast," Dana breathed. "Not soggy, not woody, not the color of fresh putty. You'll have some, won't you?"

Alison nodded. She pushed some books aside, plugging in the toaster and perching on Shelley's bed. "We're all in this together, like the man said."

"Then fill us in," Faith said, catching the first piece of toast and buttering it clear to the edges before handing it to Dana.

Alison was keeping her tone carefully light, but her eyes revealed her concern.

"You all know how strict Canby Hall policy is on lying. This is going to have to be the exception that proves that rule. An announcement is being made that Shelley and Casey have been excused from classes for health reasons, and that you two, because of living with Shelley, will be in quarantine for a few days. That will leave you free to cooperate with the authorities. It should also distract people from the fact that Shelley and Casey are gone."

"Casey gone?" Dana asked.

Alison nodded. "She went to the Inn with her parents last night. They understandably can't bear to let her out of their sight. The FBI has established a sort of headquarters there, too. We're expected down there a little later when our leaving won't be noticed. This was all worked out with Miss Allardyce, of course."

Dana breathed in slowly. Patrice Allardyce. The headmistress of Canby Hall was as much a terror as a mystery to her. It wasn't that she was mean — on the contrary, she was just so precise and elegant that she made everyone feel like an awkward clod around her. The headmistress's dedication to the rules of Canby Hall was famous. Just knowing that Miss Allardyce had been consulted about Shelley deepened Dana's fear.

"What about Shelley's family?" Faith asked.

"They're expected in tonight," Alison replied. Then she said with reproach, "Faith, you aren't eating."

Faith grinned. "Everybody has hang-ups, I guess," she admitted. "But I can't stand food until I've brushed my teeth."

Alison checked her watch. "In a few minutes the halls will be emptied for first period classes, then you can go."

Dana's toast caught in her throat. *Where was Shelley? What kind of breakfast was she getting? If any at all.*

"You know there are eight days until that trial," she reminded Alison as Faith shot down to the bathroom with her toothbrush and towel.

"We just have to think of one day at a time," Alison told her. "Everyone is doing everything they can."

The snow was three inches deep by the time they drove to the Inn in Alison's little car. It was a Christmas snow, no drifts, only puffs like cotton clinging to every twig, and the sun a hazy paleness through the steadily falling flakes.

Casey sat like a fair shadow as the investigators went through the previous day in tedious detail. Then, when Dana thought the interview was surely over, one of the men rose and turned on a machine.

"Now I want you to listen to this very carefully. I will run it through twice without stopping. Sometimes it helps to close your eyes. What you are listening for is any recognition of this voice."

Dana realized the palms of her hands were suddenly wet. On the recording a telephone rang — once, twice, three times. Then after a click, she heard the recording of Casey's father's voice.

The quality of the recording was familiar. After Dana's parents had separated and her mother was away on business so much of the time, she had installed a recorder on the family phone. It had worked very well. Even if Dana couldn't reach her mother, she could always leave a message so her mother would know to call.

"This is Jason Flint. I am unable to come to the phone at this time, but if you will give the time, the date, your name, and number at the sound of the tone, I shall return your call as soon as possible."

After the silence was broken by a musical tone, a man's voice spoke, strangely muffled:

"The time is midnight, February twenty-first. You don't need to answer this call. We have your daughter. No harm will come to her before the day of the trial. When the charges against Broderick Ames are dropped, she will be released unharmed. If you testify against Broderick Ames, you will never see her alive again."

Without comment the agent rewound the tape and played it through a second time. Strangely, the words held even more impact the second time through. And they all heard sounds of water.

The machine snapped off. One by one Dana and Faith shook their heads.

"Nothing at all?" the agent asked.

"Nothing," Dana said. "I've never heard a voice like that. There was something strange about it."

"Probably a handkerchief over his mouth," the agent explained. "But he would only do that if his voice might possibly be recognizable to someone."

Mr. Flint was sitting dejectedly, staring at the floor. "Neither my wife nor I had even a glimmer," he said quietly.

The phones had been ringing steadily in the next room. The agent rose. "If you will excuse us now. Thank you for your effort. We prefer that you stay here today just in case something comes up that we need your help with."

The room that Casey's parents had reserved at the Inn was a large double suite that overlooked the village common. Mrs. Flint invited them in with a smile. "Hardly all the comforts of home, but maybe you girls can stand it for a day. Fortunately, the Inn has agreed to provide room service so we can have lunch up here in the room."

Mr. and Mrs. Flint came and went to the suite down the hall where the agents had set up their office. Casey sat dejectedly, making no effort to rouse from her thoughts. Faith fiddled with the TV dial and got one soap after another.

"I've got enough grief of my own," Casey growled. "Who needs them?"

For what had to be about the millionth time in the months since she had known Faith, Dana was surprised by her friend's capable handling of a difficult situation. There wasn't any way that the three of them could bear to go through a long day cooped up in that room without someone exploding.

Sensing this, Faith turned from the TV and curled up in a chair with her slender arms around her legs.

"Now," she said brightly. "Someone suggest a game we can play."

"Play," Casey wailed as if insulted. "How can you even talk about playing when Shelley —"

Faith interrupted her firmly.

"I can talk about playing because there is nothing for us to do except keep from brooding ourselves into tears. Any minute one of those agents might come in here with a question or a request, and we'll need our minds sharp and our moods good enough to help him."

"But it's my fault," Casey wailed. "It's all my fault."

"Naturally," Faith said briskly. "Knowing that you were to be kidnapped, you cleverly managed to get your good friend Shelley —"

"Stop that," Casey howled.

"Then stop that other silliness," Faith snapped back at her. "Now, I have a deck of cards — what do you want to play?"

"Mom always carries cards, too," Casey volunteered.

"Good," Faith said. "With two decks we can play Spite and Malice."

For three healthy girls who had had absolutely no exercise all morning, they managed to put away an astonishing amount of lunch. The crock of onion soup that Dana ordered was thickly capped with melted cheese. She was warmed by the food and was drowsy enough to drop out of the game and watch Faith keep Casey distracted through the long, endless hours.

The snow stopped a little after four. Children appeared like mushrooms on the common below the window. They built a snow fort in front of the old cannon and started hefting the beginning of a snowman up on a cement bench.

Mr. and Mrs. Flint joined them for tea, hot raisin scones, and little sandwiches of cucumber and smoked salmon.

"This came just in time," Casey told them. "We've run out of games to play."

"Just card games," Dana corrected her. "We haven't even played Shelley's favorite yet."

She hadn't realized that the name would darken the room as it did. Mr. Flint spoke swiftly in the sudden silence. "Tell us Shelley's favorite game. I'd like to play it, too."

Dana winked hard against the tears behind her eyes. "We started doing it in bed because sometimes none of us are sleepy when the lights go out. It's really out of *Through the Looking Glass*. You begin with the first letter of the alphabet. We call it 'I Love My Love.' "

"I know that," Mrs. Flint said. "Or rather I did when I was little."

"Try," Faith urged.

Mrs. Flint looked like Casey when she squinched her face up.

"Let's see, I love my love with an *A* because she is . . . *adorable*. Her name is *Annabell* and she . . ."

"Lives in a . . ." Dana prompted.

Mrs. Flint nodded. "She lives in an *anthill* and eats *avocados* and *artichokes*."

"Me next," Mr. Flint insisted. "I love my love with a *B* because she is *boisterous* . . ."

Casey insisted on *C* and Faith got Dana's letter.

They were going through the alphabet for the second time when the agent called Mr. Flint to the door to tell him that Shelley's parents had arrived.

"We all look alike," Faith said in the car as Alison drove them back to Baker House. "We all have the same look of shock in our eyes. We've got to *do* something."

Alison nodded in the darkness. "Look what you've done already. Just keeping Casey from beating herself to death with guilt all day was valuable. And going into Shelley's parents arms the way you did had to help them. Tomorrow you have to start back to classes. You can worry about Casey and Shelley being 'laid up' but don't give anything away. Can you manage that?

"Oh," she added as she parked the car. "There's one more important thing you two can do. Casey's parents have to leave tomorrow. We are going to smuggle Casey up to the penthouse to stay until we locate Shelley. You might want to bring some of her things up there so she'll feel more at home. And again, girls, thanks a lot."

"More than that," Faith told Dana as they let themselves into their quiet room. "I don't know what we can do, but surely we can do more than what Alison suggests."

CHAPTER
SEVEN

Dana dreaded going back to the room that she and Faith had shared with Shelley all these months. Once there, she found it even worse than she had feared. It was impossible to raise her eyes without seeing something that brought Shelley back with a painful thud. The snow, which had glowed with a soft radiance from inside Alison's car, drifted past the windows with a dreary look of defeat.

Dana set out her homework only to find that her mind simply couldn't stay on a single thing long enough to grasp it. She imagined a rough spot on her left thumbnail and worked at it with an emery board for a few minutes before getting up to look for a book.

She was startled by a soft chuckle from Faith's bed. She had thought Faith was reading. Instead, her roommate was lying full length with her arms behind her head, watching Dana.

"Worms in hot ashes," Faith said aloud.

"Now that really makes sense," Dana told her. "Who's a worm in hot ashes?"

"You are," Faith said, swinging to a sitting position in one smooth motion. "To be more accurate, we both are. I can't settle down here, and clearly you are having the same problem."

Dana shrugged, unable to contradict her.

"So," Faith said brightly, reaching for her shoes. "I have made up a rescue operation for two hot worms — you and me."

At Dana's questioning glance, she explained. "Alison says that we are to report for classes tomorrow. Since Casey will be spirited up to the penthouse sometime tomorrow, we should take her things up there tonight. That will get us out of the room for a while."

"Good idea," Dana agreed. "Won't we need a list?"

Faith grinned at her. "You might need a list. Casey might even make a list. I would simply gather up the basics. Surely she took her toothbrush and all that with her when she went to the Inn. The same for makeup, although I'm not sure that Casey even wears any."

Dana was on the point of mentioning that Casey hadn't until she started trying to look like Shelley. Casey's freckles were a whole different look from Shelley's smooth, fresh face. Fortunately Dana caught herself in time.

"Underwear," she said hastily.

"And a change of sweaters and jeans." Faith nodded.

Dana looked thoughtfully around the room. "Maybe we'll think of other things when we get up there."

By leaving the door ajar to listen until the hall was clear, they managed to make their way to Casey's single room without running into anyone. Once inside, Faith muttered angrily to herself, "Wouldn't you know? We forgot to bring anything to carry the stuff upstairs in."

Dana had opened Casey's closet door to peer inside.

"That should be no problem," she said. "Look at those wooden boxes, aren't they neat?" The entire floor of Casey's closet was filled with sturdy, slatted wooden crates. On the shelf above the hangers was another row of the same boxes. None had labels on them, but it was easy to see what each box contained.

"Great, aren't they?" Faith agreed. "I've seen them here before. I even meant to ask where she got them. They are really unusual and a nice upward step from my cardboard orange boxes."

Dana, kneeling to sort out socks, grinned

up at her. "Oh, I don't know. I sort of like that painted Florida orange in a baseball cap that grins up at me every time your door is open."

By putting shorts in with the T-shirts, Dana made an empty box for the things they were collecting. With underclothes, shirts, socks, jeans, and an extra pair of pajamas all folded into the crate, Dana sat back on her heels with a frown.

"Cards," she said aloud. "Her mother might keep hers at the Inn. I'd play a lot of solitaire if I were caught up there."

"And music," Faith agreed. "If we choose the wrong cassettes, we can always switch them later."

Dana still felt an unfinished sense about the box. "You know what's wrong?" she asked Faith.

Faith shrugged. "I know what would be wrong if that box were for me. I'd have to have pictures of my family and the penguin with the floppy bill that I've had since the seventh grade. I'd need those nice grown-up substitutes for a snuggly blanket. Surely Casey has those kinds of things."

Dana had opened Casey's desk drawer and added a sketchbook and drawing pencils. She turned to Faith very quickly. "Of course. The things we are missing here are the things up there in your closet. That Casey had thrown away. I bet her special things are in that big green trash bag."

"Hey," Faith agreed softly. "How could I have forgotten, when even my tennis shoes have gotten claustrophobia from being so cramped in there? But let's take this stuff up and warn Alison that we might have another trip."

They were barely back into their room before someone rapped at the door.

"Telephone for Dana Morrison," the muffled voice said. "It's Bret Harper from Oakley Prep. He insists that he has to speak to Dana."

Dana stared at Faith a long moment.

"It wouldn't hurt to talk to him," Faith suggested.

"Yes it would," Dana told her. "He has already asked me to the supper dance at his school this coming Friday night. I promised him I'd let him know. Now I can't explain why I can't go."

Faith went to the door.

"Dana can't come to the phone now," she called to the girl outside. "Please just tell Bret that Dana can't be reached by phone."

"Well," the voice hesitated. "Okay, but he was really insisting."

"Just insist right back," Faith told her. "And thanks a lot for the call."

Faith had to take almost all of her clothes out to get the big green trash bag out of the back of her closet.

"What a way to handle good things," Dana told her, a little shocked at the bulky bag tied at the neck.

"Listen," Faith reminded her. "This is a lot better treatment than they were going to get in the trash compacter."

When they sorted out the contents of the bag, it was mostly letters and postcards and family snapshots. Instead of a floppy billed penguin there was a sadly overweight owl who leaned on one wing and stared solemnly at them. The biggest item was a long photo album held together with a knotted boot thong. The only framed picture was all the way at the bottom, and the glass had been broken. Jagged triangles of glass spilled out on the floor when Faith tried to lift it out.

"What a shame," Dana said.

"And it's such a good picture of her dad," Faith agreed.

The color photograph had been taken on a dock with a big boat being loaded in the background. Small clouds scudded in an intensely blue sky, and every color of banner fluttered from the ship. From the grainy texture of the print, Dana guessed it had been blown up from an ordinary snapshot. It had been matted with a white board decorated with a blue line the same shade as the sky. The figure of Mr. Flint covered most of the scene, lifting him from the crowd on the dock. He was carrying a dark leather briefcase, and the sunlight glinted on that beautiful white hair as he waved at whoever was holding the camera.

"I hate to have her see this all broken,"

Dana said, remembering the tenseness in Mr. Flint's face when they had left him at the Inn.

"Listen," Faith said. "This frame is a standard size. That means that we can buy glass for it without having it specially cut or anything."

"So?" Dana asked, carefully picking up the broken pieces of glass and tucking them into an envelope.

"So after school tomorrow I have to pick up the pictures from Parent-Alumnae Weekend for the *Canby Clarion*. There were so many that we had them developed at the studio downtown instead of trying to run them all through the darkroom. The photo lab is only a couple of blocks from that good lumber yard where we bought the cork for our bulletin boards. I'll get the glass for this, and Casey can have it by tomorrow evening."

"Great," Dana said. "And we'll split the cost, right?"

Faith nodded and grinned at her.

Early in their friendship Dana realized that her allowance was easily twice what Faith had to run on. Only once did she make the mistake of trying to pick up Faith's part of a bill.

Faith had straightened her out fast.

When Faith was annoyed her voice lost its playful tone and became almost silken. "Look, Dana," she had said quietly. "I pay my way or I don't fly. The pizza I can't afford is the pizza I don't eat, right?"

"Right," Dana had replied, wishing she had never reached for the check.

Faith replaced the letters and the album in the sack and put it back into her closet. Then, cross-legged on the rug, she carefully pulled out the jagged triangles of glass that still clung under the wooden edges of the frame.

Even after she was through she sat studying the picture. When Dana leaned over to see what she was looking at, Faith shook her head.

"I was just trying to imagine how it would be to live the kind of life that Casey's parents do."

"The art museums and all that?" Dana asked.

Faith nodded. "And the traveling. See how comfortable and at home he is there in some foreign port? That's so far, so strange, so different from the life I know that it might as well be on a different planet."

"And the language," Dana agreed. "Sometimes Mother and I shop over in the United Nations Building. All around us are people talking in languages that we can't even identify, much less understand."

Faith shrugged and set the picture on the table. "Maybe I would feel the same way in Shelley's world. Do you know that the only time I saw corn growing was from a train window when I was on my way here?"

Dana laughed. "I know that feeling. The

only horse I ever patted before coming to Canby Hall was hitched to a hansom cab in Central Park."

"They are going to know that Shelley isn't Casey Flint," Faith said suddenly. "The way her words come out, the way she thinks. There is a lot of difference between her and Casey."

Dana laid her hand on Faith's knee. "Listen. There's one thing we can't afford to do. We can't let our imaginations run wild about Shelley. We have to keep a firm hold on ourselves. Tomorrow we're going to be out there with everybody looking at us and staring and asking questions. One accidental lapse into tears, and we'll have failed Shelley."

The knock on the door was imperative this time.

"Listen, Dana Morrison," the same girl shouted. "I've been waiting for a call all evening and every time the phone rings it's that Bret Harper of yours. Put him out of his misery and let some of the rest of us get our calls in."

"But I don't want to talk to him," Dana protested. "I really can't."

"You have to," the girl said angrily. "Mrs. Betts on the switchboard said for you to take that call. She says he's wearing her ear out."

Faith was no help. She only lifted her shoulders in an elaborate shrug.

"Okay," Dana submitted. "I'll take the call on the hall phone."

"Well, please be quick about it," the girl snapped.

The angry girl had disappeared by the time Dana got out into the hall. Dana was glad she hadn't recognized the voice. If she was lucky, the girl's call would come and she would forget her annoyance at Dana.

Bret was irritated enough. She heard it in his first word of greeting.

"Well, finally," he said.

"Finally," she told him in a firm tone, hoping he would drop that line right away.

"What in the world is going on there, anyway?" he challenged. "I considered calling the Kremlin direct to see if that was any harder than getting Dana Morrison on the phone."

Dana laughed, wishing she knew only one convincing phrase in Russian. Then she said, "I'm really sorry, Bret. It is just one of those times."

Her tone seemed to soothe him. "Well, baby, I was getting a little panicky. I need to firm our reservations for the buffet supper."

"Money up front and all that?" she asked.

"Come on, Dana," he coaxed. "It's just that I've looked forward to this for so long. You had that big weekend last week. Think how long it has been since I've seen you. You are coming with me, aren't you?" Then as if he were afraid of her answer, he chattered on with a big sales talk about what a great buffet there would be and what good music was planned.

He was still describing the band when she finally broke in. "Listen, Bret. It sounds wonderful, and there's nothing I'd rather do than go with you, but I really can't."

The silence was ominous.

"Are you going home to New York?" he asked.

That caught Dana off guard. "Not exactly," she said.

"Then do you want to explain why you can't go when you want to so much?" His voice was suddenly terribly calm.

"Yes," she said impulsively. "I really want to explain, but I can't. This is something you really have to take on faith."

"You want to explain but you can't," he responded, his tone suddenly acid. "A matter of life or death, I suppose."

Dana shut her eyes against the sudden heat of tears. She was the one who had cautioned Faith against letting their imaginations run wild, against betraying the situation with sudden tears. The tears were streaming down her own face and she felt that hard, painful place in her chest that always came with thoughts of Shelley and what could be happening.

"Something like that," she whispered to Bret through her tears. "Something very much like that."

"Dana," he said, suddenly concerned.

"Trust me, Bret," she begged. "Just trust me."

Because of the tears, she hung up quickly and stood there a long minute before going back to Faith.

CHAPTER EIGHT

When Shelley hurled herself against the door and into the darkness, she heard the van screeching to a stop. Her shoulder hurt terribly when she landed and rolled desperately to escape the probing flashlight. All she got for her pains was a shoulder that ached miserably and a harsh slap across the head when he threw her back into the van.

She also saw his gun for the first time. She hadn't even thought about a gun — until the man beside the driver hitched himself around in the seat and trained it on her.

"All right, you rotten kid," he said angrily. "It's nothing to me if Flint gets you back with a hole in your head. It'll be too late by then anyway."

"Flint?" she asked in confusion.

"Don't try any smart-aleck games. He thought he was so clever getting the Feds in. Well, he forgot about you. He and the missus

84

can be pretty light-footed, but a kid like you is easy to find. He may have a warehouse of paintings to lose, but he only has one kid."

"But you're wrong," she cried. "I'm not Casey Flint."

"Sure, sure," he said, laughing shortly. "So you've got a bad memory from that fall. You better just pray that your dad doesn't develop the same problem. If he forgot about you, it would go pretty tough on one smart-aleck kid."

"I'm not Casey Flint," she repeated stubbornly. She would have gone on and told him her real name and where she was from, but the driver snorted.

"Shut that kid up, will you? It's bad enough trying to keep this thing on the road without her blathering in my ear."

The road had become rougher. The way she was being bounced around reminded Shelley of the old farm road out to the strawberry patch outside of Pine Bluff. She and her mother could never decide whether their soreness came from the berry picking or from the jostling ride along that road. It was just a collection of deep ruts that caught the wheels of her mother's station wagon and threw Shelley (and the berries) all over the seat.

In spite of trying not to, she cried when the van finally came to a stop. The man with the gun had come around and thrown something dusty and foul-smelling over her head and carried her like a bundle through the cold and into some building. Then he set her down on the floor with a thump.

"There it is, Casey Flint, your home away from home until your dad sees the light."

"I am not Casey Flint," she repeated stubbornly, trying to pull away from his grasp.

"Shut up and hold still unless you want me to leave these ropes on you," he barked at her.

"Wait," his companion said with a tinge of doubt in his tone. "You couldn't have snatched the wrong kid, could you?"

"What do you mean? This has to be Flint's kid. And she's as much of a handful as her old man is."

The other man remained unconvinced. "Where's her bag?" he asked. "Did she drop it in the van?"

"I never carry a bag," Shelley told him hotly.

"Listen to that. Like the Queen of England, this kid. Never needs money, huh?" He was laughing at her as he loosened the last of the ropes.

"Hang on," his companion said. "Check her pockets then. She wasn't going to take any cab with just that sunny smile."

Shelley tried to pull away from the hand probing in the pocket of her jacket. They found her red leather wallet with the three folded dollar bills for the cab, her lipgloss, and a comb but no identification. She had forgotten about the small brown envelope until she saw him pull it out.

"Hey, what's this?" he asked, handing it to the other man. She watched him tear open the tab and spill the delicate gold bracelet out into his hand.

The driver held the flashlight on the bracelet and turned it over. He laughed in a humorless way. "Well, that's one you didn't get away with, kid. Nice try."

"What is it?" the other man asked.

"A bracelet with the name Casey Flint engraved on it," he replied. "It says, 'Christmas, Aunt Edie, to Casey Flint.'"

Then he laughed again. "Boy, you are a little fool, aren't you? What do you think you'd be worth to anyone if you weren't your dad's daughter?"

They took the light with them when they left. Shelley waited a long time for her eyes to grow accustomed to the dimness of the room she had been left in. Her shoulder throbbed even when she tried to warm it with her other hand.

This was a country darkness, she decided. The single star that showed through the filthy window was brighter than any star she had seen in a long time, even through the cobwebs and dirt. After a while she could make out the shape of things in the room. Against the wall she could see a cot. Every bone in her body ached as she shuffled through the sawdust toward it.

Once she got herself into a position that didn't make her shoulder worse, she began to get warmer. She cried until the canvas cover of the cot was slick with her tears.

She wakened to the weak light of morning showing through the window. It was Monday.

She lay quietly a long time, staring around the room and trying to believe what had happened to her. If she were going to be a prisoner, she had only one important thing she could do. She could keep track of time because surely with every day that passed someone would be closer to rescuing her.

She thought of her digital watch with the calendar that was carefully stored in the jewelry case in her room. The watch had been a going-away present from her brothers when she left for Canby Hall. When the battery had run out, she'd meant to have it replaced at once. Instead, it kept slipping her mind every time she was in the village until she got used to being without it. What she wouldn't give for the gleaming face of that little watch right now.

She was being held in a high, narrow room with that single window set in the wall. Under the best of circumstances the window was too small to admit much light. And this was surely the dirtiest window she had ever seen. Ropes of old cobwebs draped against the weak light, heavy with dust.

There were no signs of new spiders at least. But what sensible spider would stay in a place like this where there was not even enough warmth to keep a fly buzzing?

She was horrified to see how filthy the blanket was that she had crept under so hastily in the dark. If there were even a hint of warmth in the room she wouldn't let that thing close to her. If only she had warmer clothes. Because she had planned to travel by cab both ways to the railway station and back, she hadn't changed her clothes before she and Aunt Edie left. She would have given up her lightweight wool skirt and jacket forever if she could only slide her legs into nice warm pants.

The only furniture in the room besides the cot was a bench just inside the door. Her captors had set a pitcher of water there with a basin and a smudged glass. The floor was an uneven drift of sawdust discolored by time and smelling of dirt.

By exploring, she discovered that a rough door in the corner of the room opened onto a narrow stall. There was no light at all in that closet-sized room. A blackened toilet without a lid stood against the wall beneath an overhead tank. A chunk of wood fastened to a rope served to operate the flush mechanism. She wondered that the water in the tank didn't freeze. If possible, this little room was even colder than the larger one. The wooden wall was so poorly joined that a chill draft swept in between the boards to swirl around her ankles.

The man who opened the door was masked. She realized that there must be heat in the next room from the surge of warm air that came when he stuck a carton of milk and a sack on the bench inside the door. He slammed back into the other room without speaking to her.

The milk was fine and the sticky buns in the sack better than nothing. Eating cross-legged on the bed, huddled under the blanket, she decided they were holding her in an old abandoned sawmill. For a few minutes she felt awfully clever at having figured that out. Then she was even able to laugh at her conceit. How Paul would have roared at her Sherlock Holmes act.

"Amazing," he would say. "You are out in the country at the end of a rough road. The place smells like the fresh logs that your dad brings in for the fireplace. There's sawdust everywhere, even in the spiderwebs, and the sound of a waterfall to run the wheel. Marvelous, my dear Holmes. How do you perform these feats of deduction?"

There was still the problem of keeping track of time. In every book she had read about prisoners, they had kept some tally of the passing days by making marks of some kind, usually on a wall.

There was nothing in the room to make a mark with. Even if there had been, the walls were so crudely finished that nothing less than a deep cut would have left a mark.

By the time she wakened the second morning, huddled inside that filthy blanket, she had figured out a plan. Forcing herself out of the warmth of the cot, she kneeled and cleared a space on the floor under her cot. She marked the two days — Monday and Tuesday — with two tiny heaps of sawdust.

It was clear at once that controlling her imagination was going to be even harder than keeping track of time. The days seemed to stretch forever, with only her meals to break the monotony. The milk and sticky buns turned out to be the best food of the day. Lunchtime brought a sandwich and French fries with a cola, and the night the same. Everything was so cold that the top of her mouth felt a little greasy all the time.

She thought about exercising but couldn't force herself from the warmth of the blanket that long. In the end, she made a game of going home in her mind. By concentrating, she could picture every room of her home back in Pine Bluff. She worked at it until she could see every piece of furniture in a room and what was on it. The kitchen was the hardest because it was there that she and her mother spent the most time together. She couldn't picture the refrigerator without seeing her mother turn from the open door with that bright, warm smile. The round table in the breakfast nook brought instant tears. She could see her father peering over his paper to laugh at something one of the boys had said and Jeff slipping a bite of bacon to the cat under the table.

She had to force her mind away from the mill to keep from thinking what those men would do when they discovered that she really wasn't Casey Flint. If it hadn't been for the bracelet that Aunt Edie had handed her, she might not even be alive now.

By the disappearance of the light on the second day, Shelley had decided one more thing. One of the first things she had heard at Canby Hall was how horrible the food was. The meal that the girls talked about the most was called Slime and Slide. Shelley had never really been able to get it to go down her throat; it looked perfectly nauseating. But here in this icy prison, she looked back at the food of Canby Hall wistfully. Compared with what she was living on here, the Canby Hall cooks produced four-star cuisine.

Aside from the little piles of sawdust, she had managed to improvise a primitive toothbrush from some tape she tore off the inside hem of her jacket. It wasn't a thing of beauty, but wrapped around a small piece of wood, it worked better than nothing.

On the day that she knew must be Wednesday, she worked a long time getting the tangles out of her hair and brushed her teeth carefully after every one of the sacks came and was devoured. The same kind of low-level anger that used to help her win swimming meets was coming to her assistance. It wasn't that she ever hated or resented the girls she swam against. It was more that she had a stubbornness that wouldn't let anything defeat her.

She had heard rumbling voices from beyond the wall from the first. But clinging to the cot, she had been unable ever to make out a single word.

Now, with this new stubbornness, she found a place against the wall where she could huddle in the blanket and catch a few words now and then.

They played cards a lot. The one that was losing was hardly a good sport. He cursed and scraped his chair in anger. She began to know when food was coming by the grinding of the van's gears outside as it departed and returned. That meant some town was near enough to provide that endless succession of grease-stained bags.

On Wednesday night, she heard the word "Melrose" twice when the men were talking. Vaguely she remembered seeing that word on a map. She thought about the name Melrose and the map of Massachusetts as she drifted off to sleep.

On Thursday, she realized that she had been wrong in her original deductions. This must be a sawmill all right, but it certainly wasn't abandoned. Early that morning, she heard the sound of a truck outside and men talking. A few minutes later she leaped from the cot at the screeching whine of a saw ripping through lumber. It seemed to go on for hours, starting and stopping. Her ears ached from the vibration echoing from the walls.

When the mill fell silent again, she heard the men say something about Melrose. One of the men was angry enough to curse Jason Flint in a loud, angry voice. "I never get a thing but that darned recording."

His words brought a sudden flood of tears. Casey was always complaining about her parents being off in Europe or somewhere when she needed them. *What if Mr. Flint were in Belgium or Spain or one of those places? What if they had never gotten the message that these men thought they were holding Casey Flint? But the people at Canby Hall must know she was missing! Faith and Dana would have told them.*

She was lucky to have controlled herself enough to start listening again when the man spoke in a sudden cheery tone.

"Hey, what do you know? Would you believe that I caught him this time, just as we planned? They're calling him to the phone right now."

"Remember to promise he can talk to the kid," the other man said.

The voices fell to a low mumble. Even with her ear against the wall Shelley only caught an occasional phrase.

"Hey," she heard, and then something about "trust."

"Can we trust her?" That was what he had said.

The man laughed in an ugly way. "That we can manage," he said firmly.

Maybe they would really let her talk to Mr. Flint. She waited so nervously that she began to tremble. If Mr. Flint heard her voice what would he say?

"That's not my daughter."

The tears began again, worse than before. Instead of calling her to the phone, the door banged open, and the man set a sandwich and cola down, his eyes mean through the holes in the mask. That time it was a fish sandwich with something like library paste smeared over the fillet. It was terrible, but she licked the paper it had been wrapped in.

She wondered if she was getting weak. She crawled back into her cot the minute she had finished her meal. She hated herself for being dirty. She hadn't gone this long without a bath in her whole life. Her skin felt strange, dry and prickly and a little itchy. She knew that her hair would fall out if it didn't get a shampoo soon. She had to tug and tug to get it combed. When — or if — she ever got out of this place, she was going to burn the clothes she had lived in for all these days. But she kept remembering what they had said about letting her talk to Mr. Flint, and a little spiral of fear started every time she thought of it.

The worst they could do was kill her. She was probably going to die of ptomaine from that miserable food anyway. Maybe she wouldn't be taking too much of a risk if she figured out some code that she could use when she talked to Mr. Flint on the phone.

But what did she know? That she was in a sawmill? That probably that mill was somewhere near Melrose?

When Faith had something she really needed to figure out, she lay on a slant board "to make her head work better."

"Yuck," Shelley had told her.

Shelley couldn't possibly make herself lie down in that dirty sawdust. She wriggled around on the cot until she had her feet way up the side of the wall. She crossed her ankles and, her arms over her chest, wished on that single, smudged star and shut her eyes to think as hard as she could.

For a while the excitement of the plan kept her awake. Then, back under the blanket, she drifted off to sleep.

She had no idea how long she had been sleeping when the flashlight was there on her face and the man was jerking her to her feet.

"All right, come on, move it," the man said in a fierce whisper. "On your feet. Move."

Shelley smothered a moan of pain as he tugged at her sore shoulder. The light she had been so startled by was suddenly hidden by a piece of cloth tied tightly in back of her head.

"Just walk," he ordered. "None of that bleating, just walk."

She knew she was out of her own room because the air was warm, deliciously warm, and the floor evener. She slid a little from the sawdust clinging to her feet, and he shoved her into a chair.

"Now," he said. "Remember that gun I showed you in the van? It's right here, trained on that empty head of yours. You're going to talk to your dad. You are going to tell him that you're fine. You aren't going to pull any of your fancy tricks. When I tell you to shut up, that means you zipper your face. Got that?"

The sound of the waterfall was much more distinct in this room. It sounded a little like the sea. She heard the faint hum of a telephone ringing and a man's voice asking eagerly, "Hello? Hello?"

Shelley felt something hard and round pressed against her temple where the bandanna was tied. They were waiting for Mr. Flint to be called to the phone. The pressure of the gun was giving her a sharp, painful headache.

Then Mr. Flint was asking, "Hello. Casey? Hello."

"Oh, Dad," she said softly.

"You're crying," he said. "Are you all right?"

She could feel the impatience of the men with her. She must remember every detail of what she had planned. But her head was so foggy with sleep. She sniffed to stop the tears.

"Really all right," she insisted. "Nobody's mean to me. I get regular meals." She forced a little laugh. "Not my favorites, no mushroom soup or mashed potatoes, but I'm fed."

"Oh, Casey," he said. From his tone, Mr. Flint was as choked with emotion as she was.

"Listen, Daddy," she said swiftly. "Tell Mama-Millie that I love her. And thank Aunt Rose for the magnificent days. I'm fine, not marvelous, but fine."

"That does it," her captor grumbled. "You don't have to babble on all night.

"You did all right," he told her as he led her, still blindfolded, back into that icy room.

"Like I told you," his companion said in a satisfied tone. "Nobody can think good coming out of sleep like that. Flint will behave himself now. Wait and see, we're home free."

CHAPTER NINE

Darkness was already falling when Dana finished her last class of the day. Thursday meant choir practice. She paused on the steps of the Science Building and stared at the mist that hung along the drive and deepened as it neared the woods that lay to her right. The wishing pool in the center of the park on the campus was frozen solid, and the pale branches of the birches looked like frozen wands. From across the park the windows of the dormitories were beginning to light up as girls came back to settle down to homework in their comfortable rooms.

The other members of the choir were hurrying along with their heads down against the cold, but she couldn't make herself move. How could she stand in that warm choir room and sing with this heaviness in her chest?

Only a week ago, a bare week ago, she had

been practicing with the choir on a medley of Barry Manilow songs for the Parent-Alumnae Weekend. The program had gone off really well. As she sang, she had glanced along the table and given her mother a sly wink. She had also caught Shelley's approving glance from where she sat by Casey's Aunt Edie.

One week.

Dana frowned, trying to remember the rules about cutting choir. This was ridiculous. She had never even looked at the rules because she was so crazy about the group and felt so awfully lucky to have been selected at all. She had literally walked the floor the week of tryouts. She had stared at her ceiling all night before it was announced who had made the grade. Yet here she was thinking of skipping the meeting in which the new production would be selected. Even if she went back to Room 407, what would she do? She was tired of pretending to study while only dwelling on scary thoughts about Shelley.

Things are supposed to get easier with time, she told herself sternly. That simply wasn't true. Every day, almost every hour, she felt her fear rise about Shelley. For one thing, with every day that passed, the trial was one day closer. What was Mr. Flint going to do?

She didn't hear the thunder of the feet

down the stairs behind her until Mindy Porter roared to a stop at her side.

"Thank goodness I won't be late alone," Mindy panted. "Come on, Dana. Put on your innocent look and get a move on to choir."

Dana sighed.

Mindy's broad face was sleek with sweat. She rubbed at her cheeks with the back of a soiled mitten and grinned. "I really made time catching up with you." She kept chattering as she urged Dana along. "Some fine clear day when I am literally teetering on the brink of my grave the concept of algebra will dawn on me in a blinding series of X's and Y's streaming against the sunset sky. Move on, Dana. We're going to get chewed out if we don't hurry."

It was easier to drag along with Mindy than explain. It was easier to nod at Mindy's continuing lecture on the mystery of algebra than to get away from her and go back to her room.

They weren't really late anyway. The chatter reached them clear down the hall. Dana, in Mindy's wake, walked past Mr. Brewster, the choir director, only to be called back.

"Here, Dana," he said. "I have a note that came for you. Maybe you had better check it before I start cracking the whip on you songbirds."

The handwriting was Alison's. Dana stopped to read it before going to her place.

There was more risk there that someone might read it over her shoulder. For some unaccountable reason her hand trembled as she opened the flap.

Shelley. Maybe they had found Shelley and Alison was letting her know the first minute that everything was all right.

The spiral of hope was short-lived. Alison had written a single sentence across the folded sheet of notepaper.

"Please come to my place as soon as choir is over."

Dana looked up to see Mr. Brewster's curious eyes on her face.

"Trouble?" he asked gently.

Dana shook her head and forced a smile as she thrust the note in her pocket.

Mr. Brewster laughed softly. "Then I'd say that you have a pretty guilty conscience to read a house parent's note with that expression on your face." He turned away at once, raising his voice. "Girls," he called. The clamor diminished as Dana made her way to her place.

The next choir program would be the spring concert. Dana had served on the preselection committee of three. She was the only sophomore on the committee. Personally, she hoped that they would settle on something that hadn't been a big hit on Broadway or featured on every movie bill in the country.

"Who really wants to be compared with

Julie Andrews?" she protested when *The Sound of Music* was suggested. As for *The King and I*, nobody wanted to acquire a gleaming bald head for the lead.

Dana was only half-conscious of the conversations swirling around her. It didn't register on her what Mindy was doing when she lifted Dana's hand for a minute and quickly let it drop.

"That does it, I guess," Mr. Brewster said with satisfaction. Dana realized she had just voted for something. "I really expected you prima donnas to give me more fight. The scores will be in your mail slots on Saturday. We will audition on Tuesday for the individual parts."

Tuesday. Tuesday, March first. Dana swallowed hard to keep her breathing even. The trial would begin on March first.

"What did we decide on?" Dana asked Mindy as they put their wraps back on.

"A lot you cared," Mindy laughed. "Now you can just wait and see what lands in your box Saturday."

The mist had deepened into a full-scale fog. It hung a little way above the ground so that the trees seemed to float in the air, rootless. Had Faith gotten the same note from Alison? Mindy was laughing about something she herself had said. She was dragging along now, still complaining about the way she was being wrestled to the ground by algebra.

"I need to pep it up a little," Dana told her. "I am really in kind of a rush."

"A fog is what you're in," Mindy corrected her, watching her go on ahead with a puzzled look.

Dana bolted through the hall and up the stairs to her room. Faith's coat was across the bed along with a stack of books. Dana found herself breathless by the time she got to Alison's door and was let in.

At first, Dana didn't recognize the man in the striped overalls. Having only seen him in his suit, it didn't dawn on her that this plumber in a billed cap was one of the investigators from the Inn.

He grinned at her. "A little problem with the drainage up here," he explained. Then more seriously, "We felt I might create less curiosity coming in this way."

The tension in the room was almost visible. Casey was buried in the pillows, her knees drawn tightly against her chest and her eyes dull from the strain of the past days. Faith turned from the window as Dana came in. She winked that slow way that was more like a pat on the shoulder.

They had obviously been waiting just for Dana. The agent pulled a tape from his plumber's bag and set it into the machine.

"Like before," he said tersely. "Twice through all the way, and then we'd like any reaction you have."

There was the ring of the phone and the stranger's voice, the same voice, asking to speak to Jason Flint. Dana thought she was hearing soft music, the tinkle of glass, and a woman's easy laughter.

"Enjoying the party, Flint?" the man asked as Mr. Flint, sounding a little amazed, said hello.

"No chatter," the man went on without an answer. "I don't intend to give you time to trace this call. Here's your friend."

At the sound of Shelley's voice, Dana felt her lungs empty of air. A glance at Faith confirmed that she had the same horrified reaction. Shelley sounded drugged, her voice thick and strange.

And the words she said were crazy, not the way Shelley usually talked at all. The gentleness in Mr. Flint's questions only seemed to make it harder for Shelley to speak. And the answers were really odd.

A movement caught Dana's eye. Casey was groping for a pencil and paper, trying to get the words down. Usually so in control, she looked increasingly astonished as the words went on.

"They've given her something," Faith said angrily the moment the recording stopped.

The agent nodded. "Anything else?"

"She's got my aunt's name wrong," Casey said. "It's Aunt Edie, not Aunt Rose."

"And she hates mashed potatoes with a

passion," Faith blurted. "As for mushrooms, she's terrified of them."

"They haven't given her anything that will hurt her, have they?" Casey whispered.

The agent shook his head. "Probably just a sedative to keep her mind from being sharp enough to send a message." Then, glancing at Casey, "Do you all want copies of this?"

"Oh, yes," Casey said. "I missed that noise that was always there before, you remember."

He nodded and pulled out typescripts of the tape for each of them. "The sound of the sea. We're still working on that."

He didn't seem disappointed by the meager response. He merely repacked his bag and rose. "Don't feel bad. None of us had high hopes for it when we heard it. But it was worth a try."

"If there were sea sounds, then they were drowned out by other noises," Casey went on thoughtfully. "Where did this one get taped?"

"That is our best clue so far. Mr. and Mrs. Flint were attending a private art party in Boston. Only people in the art world knew of the party. We even had to argue with Mr. Flint about having the recorder put on his host's phone because so few people knew they would be there."

Casey flashed with anger. "They went to a party?" she cried, jumping to her feet. "They went to a party while Shelley is off somewhere we don't even know?" Her voice broke in fury.

"Dana and Faith are going to their regular classes," Alison reminded her. "Do you think they want to be doing that? Everything must be kept as normal as possible on the surface."

Casey stared at her before fleeing to the bathroom.

"Remember," the agent said from the door. "If anything at all comes to you, report it to Miss Cavanaugh and she'll get in touch with us."

When he was gone, Faith stood uncertainly. "Do you think Casey is all right?" she asked with concern.

Alison nodded. "She just can't bear to have people see her cry."

Faith sighed. "Listen. Tell her I have to pick up the pictures and make the layout deadline for the *Canby Clarion*. The man is picking it up about six. Tell her that I'll come up and spend some time with her as soon as I get through."

Alison nodded and looked at Dana. "I really hate leaving her alone as much as I have to."

"I can stay right now," Dana told her. "I even brought her homework assignments in case she wanted to work on them."

By the time Faith got back a little after six, Casey had done most of her assignments, with Dana's support. Dana forced her mind to her own work, too. Alison's cat Doby perched between them and rumbled contentedly as he watched the waggling of Casey's pencil.

Alison rose to go down and get a dinner tray for herself and Casey. "I wish I could bring something back for you girls, too," she said. "But I'm already getting the reputation of being the biggest eater in the school because I bring double portions of everything for Casey. Will you be here when I get back?"

"Go along," Faith told her.

"I thought she would never leave," Faith hissed as soon as the door closed behind Alison. "Now come over here, both of you. I want to show you something."

As they joined her, Faith laid out some pictures on the coffee table. "Now, these aren't the best prints. I had to turn the originals in so I just xeroxed these." The pictures were the shots from the weekend just past. There was a good shot of the big banquet with the headmistress, Patrice Allardyce, making a point of some kind with an upraised hand. Only Shelley's fair hair showed at Aunt Edie's side as she leaned over the table to listen.

"Now look at this one," Faith ordered. The excitement in her voice brought their heads together over the photostat.

"Who are we looking for?" Casey asked after a second.

"Somebody whose face you recognize," Faith replied a little impatiently.

"But I know half of the kids in that picture," Casey protested.

"No, no," Faith said. "Somebody else. Somebody besides one of the girls."

Dana gasped. "The man," she cried. "That is the man in the background of the foreign picture of Mr. Flint."

Casey stared at them blankly.

"Casey hasn't seen the rest of that picture," Faith reminded Dana. "I wanted her to see this before I showed her the other one. The mat covers him when it is framed."

Casey yelped when Faith took the framed picture of her father and started to dismantle it. "Stop, what are you doing?" she challenged Faith.

"This," Faith said with a flourish. With the matting removed, the picture was as Dana remembered it: the side of the ship, the posts wound with rope, and behind Mr. Flint, watching him as he waved, was the same man who appeared in two of the pictures from Parent-Alumnae Weekend.

"I have seen him," Casey said thoughtfully. "I have seen that man before, but it might have been a long time ago or in some other sort of place."

The room was suddenly silent. "Don't you think we should show these to Alison even if we don't know who he is?"

"Of course," Dana replied. "There's even a good chance that Mr. Flint will recognize him. We have to try anything we can to help Shelley."

The girls had their written transcription of

Shelley's conversation with Mr. Flint. Dana
stared at her copy on the table and shook her
head. "So much is happening at once that
maybe this will be solved. There are those
pictures, and we actually heard Shelley."

"But so strange," Casey said. "Shelley
sounded so strange."

Faith was leaning over the script, too,
looking at it with narrowed eyes.

"She must have been under a sedative,"
Dana said dully. "You can't pay attention to
how someone talks under those conditions."

Faith was staring at Dana with the strang-
est look on her face. Before she could speak,
Alison rapped on the door with the tray, and
Casey let her in.

They barely let Alison put the tray down
before showing her the pictures. They were
still explaining when Alison reached for the
phone and started to dial. "No," she said
aloud to herself. "I won't take that chance."
Then, "I'm going down to the Inn to see the
Flints. They've come back, but Casey was to
stay here.

"Listen, you two," she said, turning to Dana
and Faith. "Run to the dining hall and get
your dinners over fast so you can get back up
here." Her voice broke on the words. "Oh,"
she sighed. "Wouldn't it be wonderful to get
a break . . . just any break?"

Out in the hall Faith grabbed Dana by the
arm.

"Who do you know that can drive a car?" she asked.

"Almost all the seniors," Dana replied.

Faith shook her head impatiently. "No. I mean someone who can drive a car and could get a car for us."

"Bret," Dana remembered. "He drives a beat-up old station wagon on our dates."

"Then call him," Faith ordered. "Tell him you want to go to the Friday night dance, and he has to have his car. You can get us both checked out for Friday night, can't you? For that dance?"

"Faith," Dana cried. "You know there's a signed permit for you to go home with me. But I can't just call Bret up and invite myself after I've turned him down. And tell him I'm bringing a friend, too. And talk about nerve — who can ask a boy for a date only if he has wheels?"

"Okay," Faith said. "Forget about me. I can manage somehow. Go get that date reinstated and with a car. I'll race down and get some food while you call."

"But I don't understand," Dana wailed.

"The game," Faith whispered. "I think that Shelley was giving us clues in the form of our game. I don't have them all figured out but I'm sure, Dana, really sure."

"What about the FBI?" Dana asked. "They have cars."

Faith shook her head. "It's too much of a

long shot. They'd think we were crazy. Quit wasting time and call Bret."

Faith was off down the stairs two at a time, leaving Dana staring after her in confusion.

The game. That meant "I Love My Love." Dana shook her head and got some change for the pay phone. Bret was going to give her a hard time over this. And he had a right to. This was something she would never live down with Bret. But Faith seemed so sure.

CHAPTER TEN

Dana stood in the phone booth with all her fingers crossed, waiting for Bret to be called to the phone. *Let this be easy,* she begged. *Just let be this be easier than I think it will be.*

She heard someone shouting his name along the hall, the sound of running feet, and then what sounded like a scuffle at the phone. When his greeting came, it sounded breathless.

"That you, Bret?" she asked, a little unsure.

"Hey, Dana." His tone was clearly delighted. "It's me, all right. These clowns fight you to the ground for every phone call."

"It must be great to be so popular," she told him.

"It's not that at all," he laughed. "Every time a girl calls, they treat it like the end of the world."

Dana felt herself tense in the darkness of the phone booth. She told him, unable to force much lightness into her tone, "Well, I'm asking a guy for a date."

The silence seemed overly long. "Anybody I know?" he finally asked.

She hesitated. "Let's see. How about five foot ten, dark curly hair, with a terrific smile, of course? Oh, and I forgot. His initials are BH."

"Whew." He laughed as if relieved. "For a while there you were describing the entire Oakley lacrosse team. This *is* for the dance Friday night, I hope. Or I could be there in thirty minutes."

"The dance tomorrow night is fine, more than fine." She paused. "You will have your car, won't you?"

His tone grew confused. "I'll have the heap, all right. What's up, Dana? You really don't sound like yourself."

"I hate to fall back on this, Bret," she admitted. "But I guess I'll have to ask you to trust me."

"No problem there, Dana," he said. "I'll pick you up about seven."

"That's fine." Then she paused. "What would happen if I brought a friend?"

"Five feet ten, dark curly hair, terrific smile?" he asked.

"You are now describing my roommate Faith Thompson."

"Faith," he said. "Super! There's always a bunch of guys who haven't managed to get a date. She'll get swept off her feet."

"Thanks, Bret," Dana sighed. "More than you can imagine."

"I'm the one to be thanking you," he told her. "See you tomorrow."

Anyone who didn't know Faith would have thought she was studying when Dana went back to their room. She sat primly at her desk. The supper she had brought back for Dana was on Shelley's bed. Faith was staring at her notebook, a pencil twirling between her fingers. Dana knew she couldn't be studying. Faith had a theory that all information had to be acquired by the use of gravity. She only studied on a slant board with her feet higher than her head and only then with the stereo killing the background sounds. Also, she looked up too quickly when Dana entered.

"How did it go?" Faith asked.

"As right as it could," Dana admitted. "I hate to be secretive with anyone I like as much as I do Bret. Also, it makes me feel dirty to think I am using somebody. Now come on, what is this all about?"

Faith twisted in her chair and reached for one of the sandwiches on the tray. "Now that you have us all set up, I am getting cold feet. I have been going quietly crazy ever since you left to make the call. Could my great brainstorm all be my imagination because I want to help Shelley?"

Dana was losing her patience. "Listen, Faith. I did my part. Now you have to explain why I did it before *I* go crazy."

Faith sighed. "Do you suppose that Alison is still off at the Inn?"

"She couldn't possibly have driven there and be back yet," Dana said. "You think we ought to be up there with Casey?"

Faith nodded. "Also, I think I'd like to run this theory of mine past Casey. Only don't mention Bret or the dance, okay?"

"I guess I don't have to understand to cooperate, but I *wish* I understood," Dana told her. "Let's go."

Casey, with half of her supper still uneaten, was staring into space as she petted Doby.

"We came to play a game with you," Faith said brightly.

"Thanks a lot, but I don't feel very playful," Casey told her.

"This is very serious play," Faith told her. "I want us to make up a list of the things on that recording that don't sound like Shelley."

"I don't understand this," Casey complained.

"Just do it," Faith ordered. "I'll explain in a minute."

Casey scratched her head with her pencil. "She called Aunt Edie by the wrong name."

"Rose." Faith wrote it down.

"The food is funny, just like we told the agent," Dana said. "Why would she say that she liked things that she really can't stand?"

Faith wrote "mushroom soup" and "mashed potatoes" in bold letters on her pad. "More," she prompted.

"I've never heard her call her mother 'Mama,'" Casey said with clear distaste. "In fact, I can't imagine even liking a grown girl who used that term. And anyway, her mother's name is Ann or something simple like that."

Faith wrote "Mama-Millie" on her pad.

"How about the word *marvelous*?" Faith asked.

Casey had looked up and was staring at her.

"Look at the words," Faith went on in growing excitement.

"If *M* is the letter she is trying to get us to understand, then everything would begin with that if possible," Faith said. "Look at them. Mean. Meals. Mushroom soup. Mashed potatoes. Mama-Millie. Magnificent. Marvelous. The only one that is off at all is the Aunt Rose."

"I still think the Millie is funny," Casey piped up. "There are a hundred common women's names before anyone would come up with Millie."

"But why the Rose?" Faith insisted.

Dana was staring at the dark window behind Casey. "A mill," she said suddenly. "Could somebody be kept prisoner in an old mill or something? That would explain the Millie."

"In a town named Rose!" Faith shouted. "That's it. That's the connection I couldn't get."

"Rose, Massachusetts?" Casey asked. "I never heard of it."

"A map, a map," Faith said, going through Alison's bookshelf frantically. "We need a map of Massachusetts." Then, not finding one, she turned to Dana. "Don't you have an atlas down in our room?"

Nodding, Dana let herself out and brought the book back as fast as she could clear the stairs.

"Try the index first," Faith suggested.

Dana ran her finger down the column carefully. "Roscoe, Nebraska. Rosebud, Arkansas. Rosebush, Michigan. There are Rosedales everyplace in the world except Massachusetts. Rose Hill. The nearest one of those is in Vermont."

"Mark that," Faith ordered. "And go on."

"Roseland," Dana read aloud. "There are seven of those but none close. Roselle. Rosemead. Rosemount. Rose Town. Rose Valley. Roseville. Still nothing in Massachusetts."

Faith sighed and reached for the atlas.

"Okay, we need to check the map where

we are and find something near here that makes you think of a rose. It doesn't have to be a town. It could maybe be a mountain or a river. Anything that would make you think of a rose."

They leaned over the map, studying the names of even the smallest villages. Weymouth, Cohasset, Scituate, Greenbush.

"How about that?" Casey asked, looking up.

Faith shook her head. "But leave a mark there."

"*Melrose!*" Casey yelled. "Right there, just north of here and maybe a little west."

"It looks like a pretty big town," Dana decided.

"You can have a mill almost anywhere there's a river," Faith pointed out. "See that squiggly blue line running along there? I can't find the name, but it has to be a river."

Doby leaped from his cushions and started for the door, mewing.

"Alison's coming," Casey said. "He always knows it before I can hear her."

"This isn't like the movies or TV," Faith said. "Nobody would pay any attention to this but us. So don't say anything yet, okay?"

"But how can you check it out?" Casey asked.

"I have a plan, sort of," Faith told her. "We can't do anything until Saturday. Dana and I are going to be out tomorrow night. But after that . . ."

Casey obviously was ready with a new question, but Alison was at the door with Doby rubbing a welcome around her ankles. Alison's knitted cap glistened with frost and her nose was a rosy match for her lipstick. "Brrr," she trembled. "It's a cold night out there. But it was certainly worth the trip. The Flints were so excited that they could hardly speak." She took the teakettle to the sink. "I'm having hot tea and a lot of it. Anyone want to join me?"

"We'd love to," Faith replied. "But as we were just telling Casey, Dana and I are going to be out tomorrow night and there is a lot of stuff to do."

"You will be here through the dinner hour, won't you?" Alison asked.

"I don't need to be baby-sat," Casey said a little huffily.

Alison grinned and patted her hand. "Maybe not. Maybe we just like babying you."

"We're not leaving until seven," Dana told Alison. "Maybe there will even be some word back on the pictures by then."

The minute they were back in their own room, Dana sat Faith down firmly. "Okay, friend. I've had all the mystery I can handle for a while. I'd like you to tell me why I fixed up that date with Bret."

Faith shrugged. "I didn't have it all together until just now up in the penthouse, but it was close. I decided we needed to nail down a car while we still had a chance."

"So we're going to Melrose?" Dana asked. "In that old heap of Bret's?"

Faith's eyes shadowed with doubt. "Is this all too wild?"

Dana shook her head. "Not wild, just scary. I've been thinking more about that mill. The agents were so sure that the calls were made close to an ocean. Have you ever heard the waterfall of a mill? I wonder if the sound wouldn't be a lot the same."

"See?" Faith said, brightening.

"I do see," Dana admitted. "What I don't see is how we can go to that party, find the mill at Melrose, and get back here in time to be checked in."

"Well, that's clearly not possible," Faith admitted. "But if we signed out for the weekend at your house in New York, we could sleep in Bret's car and go searching on Saturday."

Dana looked at Faith in disbelief. "Do you realize what would happen to us if we were found out?"

Faith's eyes met hers directly. "Do you realize what can happen to Shelley if somebody doesn't do something?"

"What will I tell my mother?" Dana wondered aloud.

"We could call her on Saturday. The permit slip for me to visit you in New York City is already on file," Faith reminded her.

It had been quiet in the room a long time. Dana had thought Faith was already asleep when Faith spoke quietly. "I didn't make all those clues up, did I Dana?"

"The clues are all there," Dana assured her, wishing she could be as certain as she sounded.

Because of the plan to spend the night in New York City, Dana and Faith had a good excuse to pack a bag to take with them to Oakley Prep. They decided on a single bag with woolen socks, heavy jeans, and down jackets.

"It looks as if we were going for a month." Dana laughed as they finally got the zipper shut on the two puffy jackets.

"Better than to freeze in the wilds of Melrose," Faith told her. They signed out on the weekend sheet outside of Alison's room. Then they found an unexpected line in the downstairs lobby.

"What's going on?" Dana asked Linda Patton, who was in the last place of the line.

Linda shrugged. "Apparently everybody in the whole house is going to the Oakley Prep supper dance." Then in a lower voice, "We all have to be checked out in person. And Mrs. Betts is being cross and picky about every little thing."

"That's not like her," Dana said.

"New rules or something?" Dana asked Mrs. Betts when she and Faith reached the desk.

Mrs. Betts seemed pleased to have her trouble noticed. "You might say there are new rules," she said crossly. "Everything has to be checked and double-checked for no reason at all that anyone has told me. You'd think that every girl in this building had suddenly turned into solid platinum." Her tone softened from Dana's interest. "Now, what can I do for you?"

Dana found herself breathing very deeply. "Faith and I want to check out for the Oakley Prep supper dance, and for Faith to come home with me afterward for the weekend."

Mrs. Betts's head came up sharply. "You have permission, Dana?"

Dana nodded. "Mom and I are on the phone all the time," she said, avoiding a lie as long as possible.

"But what about Faith?"

"She's come home with me before."

"You know better than that, Dana Morrison." Mrs. Betts rose and went to a file, chattering as she flipped through the names. "Unless Faith has a signed permission here to go visit you anytime, it's just plain impossible."

Faith's dark eyes held Dana's as Mrs. Betts paused.

"Ah," she said. "Here it is, all right, permission to go home to New York City with you for weekends. How will you travel?"

"Train," Dana replied. "The last train

makes a good connection in Boston." That, at least, was true.

Mrs. Betts had already put the two slips out for their signatures when she paused. "I would feel better about letting you go if you called your mother to be sure she was expecting you."

"But what if Mom isn't home right now?" Dana asked.

"Then we'll see," Mrs. Betts said impatiently, glancing at the long line of girls still waiting. "Use my phone right there."

Faith stepped aside as Dana dialed the number of her mother's apartment in New York. Mrs. Betts was signing out another girl while keeping one ear on Dana's conversation.

The phone rang four times before Dana heard the familiar click of the recorder and her mother's voice, inviting the caller to leave a message after the sound of the beep. Dana whistled softly to herself. The recorder only registered a few moments and then turned off. The trick was to manage the timing exactly.

"Hi, Mom," she said brightly when the beep sounded. "Gosh, I am glad to catch you at home." She now had a minute and a half to fill with words. "No, there's nothing wrong. It's awfully cold up here and I am sure glad I brought that down jacket. I'm taking it with me tonight."

Faith's expression was getting strained as Dana chattered on. "Oh, and we all want to thank you for the great treats that you left on Parent-Alumne Weekend. They were swell." She saw Mrs. Betts's glance of annoyance from the corner of her eye. At that moment she also heard the click of the recorder going off. "You do remember that Faith is coming home with me tonight on the late train? We'll meet you at the station. See you later."

As she hung up the phone, Mrs. Betts was signing Faith's sheet, and she reached for Dana's without another comment.

Dana and Faith left the line and took a bench where they could watch the front door. "That, my friend, was the close call of the Western world," Dana whispered.

"It's an omen," Faith told her. "A sign that what we are doing is the right thing."

CHAPTER ELEVEN

The noise level of the Baker House lobby rose to a roar as the Oakley Prep students arrived to pick up their dates for the Friday night supper dance. Dana grinned at Faith, waving a hand in front of her face. There was literally no air left as the girls, talking and smiling, walked out, leaving the air heavy with a dozen kinds of perfume.

"Like passing through the perfume department at Saks." Dana laughed.

The lobby gradually emptied as the shuttle buses filled and left for the dance. Finally only Dana and Faith were left inside the big front doors of Baker House.

Mrs. Betts, her hair awry and her glasses swinging dangerously on their beaded chain, began to sort out her office. She was mumbling to herself in an angry monotone that was totally unlike her usual manner.

At a quarter after seven, the quiet was broken by the steady blasting of a horn coming around the circle drive.

"Oh, no," Dana groaned. "That has to be Bret in that crazy car of his."

Mrs. Betts was out from behind her desk and to the door in record time. "Who is that?" she asked with annoyance, glaring through the windows. "What in the world is going on?"

Dana was struggling against an outburst of laughter. "I imagine it's my friend Bret Harper. His horn does that sometimes."

"Well." Mrs. Betts stared at the station wagon coming to a stop outside. "You girls don't put a step outside that door, that's all I can say. It's absolutely boorish to come pick up a young lady like that."

"But the horn does that," Dana tried to explain. "There's a wire loose or something."

Bret, shamefaced, was up the stairs two at a time.

"I'm really sorry to be late," he told Dana and Faith. "I stopped to get the horn fixed...." He shrugged, shouting over the blasting still coming from the car outside. "Finally I gave up."

While he was still shouting this, the horn stopped of its own accord, leaving him yelling into a sudden silence.

"Whew," he sighed, grinning at Mrs. Betts. "I hope it feels better with that out of its system."

Dana grinned to herself. Not even Mrs. Betts, in the foul mood she was in, could resist Bret's grin. "Well, young man," she began sternly. Then she grinned, too. "I will say that you know how to make an entrance."

She was still melting under Bret's smile when he apologized to her. "I can't tell you how sorry I am," he said. "I'll try to make my departure a little less dramatic."

"She's not usually such a dragon," Dana assured him as the three of them squeezed into the front seat. "This has been a slightly hysterical evening for her."

"For me, too," Bret replied. "What's up?"

Faith shrugged and Dana smiled at him. "First the dance."

"I wish I had known earlier that you were coming, Faith," Bret told her. "I could have set up a lottery and let the winner get your company as a prize."

Faith laughed softly. "I really don't want to be a drag on your evening. I could hang around in the women's lounge or something."

"Not on your life," Bret told her. "The line is already forming on the right to dance your shoes off."

"Good," Faith said. "I brought extras."

Bret, who had frowned as he put the suitcase in the backseat, didn't reply. But as he pulled out, he did cast a very thoughtful glance at his passengers.

* * *

Dana was happy to realize that Bret hadn't been exaggerating about Faith's popularity. Faith didn't sit out a single dance. When supper was served a little before midnight, Dana saw two separate plates of food being carried to Faith by glaring young men.

Bret had found a quiet corner for himself and Dana. Only when they were settled with their food did he really start quizzing Dana about her plans.

"What better time than the witching hour to discover how I rated this great evening?"

That ugly sense of guilt twisted in Dana again. She laid her hand on his arm. "Listen, Bret. You have to believe that if I could explain all this, I would. I simply can't. But Faith and I are looking for something, and we need you to help us look for it."

He stared at her, puzzled.

"It's a place," she began. "A special kind of place, and we only know roughly where it is."

"Here near Greenleaf?" he asked.

"Not really," she admitted. "It's . . . well, let me tell you what we want to do. There's no way that we could ever find it in the dark. Faith and I want to sleep in your car in the parking lot. Then tomorrow morning, as soon as you can get away, we want to go on this search. I brought plenty of money for gas, so don't worry about that."

"A sort of scavenger hunt?" he asked.

"Only deadly secret," she told him.

"Couldn't I have just taken you back to Baker and picked you up in the morning?" he asked.

She frowned. "That's funny. I didn't even think of that. I guess I was afraid something would turn up. And we need an early start, as early as possible."

"Deadly secret," he said thoughtfully. "And deadly serious, I might add." He leaned toward her and drew her close for a quick moment as he studied her face. "I believe the deadly serious and deadly secret business, Dana, because of the change in you. What I can't swallow is that you'd want me to drive you all over Massachusetts in the dead of winter because of a *place*."

Dana found that she couldn't meet his eyes.

"Are you sure it isn't a person instead of a place that has you all upset?" he pressed.

"And if it were?" she countered, looking up. "Like if it were your best friend or mine, and you were the only person in the world who could or would help?"

"Shelley," he decided. "The three best friends I know of are you and Faith and Shelley. Only Shelley isn't here."

It wasn't as if she were giving away the kidnapping. She nodded silently.

He whistled softly. "That silly little country girl."

From his tone it was clear he thought Shelley had run away. Dana stopped her own protest. She could see him weighing the day ahead against this understanding.

"I'm not the world's most experienced driver," he warned her. "And clearly the heap is not the world's best-equipped car."

She didn't mean to hold her breath but couldn't help it. All he had to do was say no. In fact, it would probably be a tribute to his intelligence if he did.

He shrugged his shoulders. "Now, I'm not doing this because it's a good idea. I'm not doing it to make a big impression on you. I'm going off on this crazy day because I'm afraid you'll manage it some other way if I don't. And then I wouldn't be there, too."

He hesitated and then asked, "If I decide not to do it, what will you do?"

"I don't know," she answered honestly.

"But you'd try something?" he asked.

"Anything I could think of," she admitted.

He shook his head. "Dana, if this crazy idea is a sample of the things you think of, I don't even want to hear about the next idea that comes up. I guess the whole school knows that Shelley is gone?"

"It's deadly secret, as I said."

He studied her a long minute. Then he kissed her lightly and got up. "The confused driver ate a hearty midnight supper. I'm going back for more lasagna. Will you come with me?"

Dana handed him her plate. "The grateful passenger joined in the pig-out," she told him, smiling into his eyes.

Bret was a mother hen, fussing over them as he settled them down in the car. He parked it clear at the back of the lot in the shadows of the trees. He even left his own down jacket with them for extra warmth.

"What if the watchman sees you?" he asked.

"We'll stay way down in the seats," Faith told him. "I, for one, don't intend to stick my head up until morning."

"Maybe not even then," Dawn yawned. "We have all the comforts of home here. Have a good night's sleep and forget about us."

"Fat chance of that," he said, dropping a quick kiss on Dana's forehead. "Sleep well."

Bret had chosen his parking place well. A clump of trees sheltered the car from the security lights that ringed the lot. It was comforting to look up and see the lighted windows of Bret's dorm go out one at a time, as the boys settled down for the night.

"Maybe now is the best time to change," Faith suggested. "That Bret is a good guy to do all this."

Wriggling out of a dress in the car was not so difficult. Getting the jeans and down jackets on proved to be more of a project. Only with the suitcase repacked did Dana

settle down to try to sleep. Faith's even
breathing told her that her roommate was
almost out for the night. Dana shifted down
in her place to follow her example. She shut
her eyes, only to open them quickly.

Madness, she told herself. She and Faith
could be expelled. And even if, by some
miracle, they located Shelley, how was she
going to explain this escapade to her mother?
The worst thing her mother ever said to her
was that Dana had a responsibility to be a
good example to her younger sister, Maggie.
What a lesson this adventure made in a
course on role modeling. Also, as hard as it
had been to get through her parents' divorce,
they had made it in one piece because nobody had ever lied to each other.

Her mother had been honest when it
really hurt. Her father had stuck to the
truth, when it made painful, white lines along
the sides of his mouth. Dana's family simply
wasn't one where people kept things from
each other. Yet here she was with a trick
recording on her mother's machine, sleeping
in the parking lot of a boys' school in the
dead of winter, and all because of some clues
(or imagined clues) from a girl who sounded
drugged.

The dark seemed to deepen as the last of
the dorm lights went out. The silence became
a hollowness that Dana strained against. The
wind stirred the trees near the car, and the

branches swayed together. They ticked softly in a random kind of rhythm. From off toward Greenleaf she heard the distant moan of a train whistle, rising and falling as it faded in the distance. That would be the late night freight. In the early days, when she still had not gotten used to Canby Hall, she had often listened to that whistle as the train passed through the nearby village and thought it the loneliest sound she had ever heard.

Dana was astonished at how deeply she was finally able to sleep. She wakened to sun streaming in through the car window and the sounds of cars and voices in the lot around them. A draft of cold air swept around as Bret unlocked the car and got in.

She giggled at his act but was honestly impressed. He was a clever conspirator. He whistled lightly to himself as he slid in behind the wheel. Not until he had kicked the motor to life and had the radio on did he speak. No one watching could have guessed that he wasn't alone in the car.

When he did speak, he affected a bad imitation of a British accent. "This is James, your chauffeur, reporting for the day's adventure. Be so kind as to direct me."

Faith giggled from the floor. "If you will be so kind as to drive west from this village." Her accent was much more convincing than his was. "And, sir, at the first sign of a possible breakfast site, stop without warning. I'm starving."

"Breakfast at your command," he replied, grinning to himself. "Posthaste, I hope, but only if I am allowed to dine with your imperial whatevers."

Dana smiled to herself. How lucky she was in her friends, and in Bret.

She and Faith stayed down until Greenleaf was behind them. They then popped up to look around.

Bret laughed. Then he stared at Faith. "What in the world do you have in your hand?"

Faith looked at him coolly. "My toothbrush and paste," she told him. "I told you I'm starving. I intend to waste no time getting into food once you find us some."

Inside the steamy little roadside café, with their faces washed and breakfast ordered, Bret stared at them across the table.

"I don't like to be nosy, but I always have more luck finding things if I know what I'm looking for."

Dana looked at Faith, who was frowning soberly.

"Do you have a map of this state?" Faith asked Bret.

Shaking his head no, he went over to the counter and spoke with the cashier. In a minute he returned. "The man said we might find one at the service station up the road a few miles."

"Never mind," Faith said, fishing in her purse.

Dana's eyes widened when she realized what Faith was unfolding on the table. "That's the map out of the atlas," she said in a surprised tone.

Faith shrugged. "My mom has an expression that you might as well be hanged for a sheep as a lamb. I wasn't sure we could get a map. I can put it back in so you'll never know it went traveling."

The waitress brought coffee and toast as Faith pored over the map, finally folding it down to only a small square that included Greenleaf and Melrose.

"Somewhere in this area" — she pointed to Melrose — "we need to find a mill."

The waitress was unself-consciously eavesdropping as she set plates of scrambled eggs in front of each of them. She craned to see the map, as she spoke up.

"What kind of mill do you want, honey?" she asked genially. "There's a lot of textile mills over by Lowell. And down there," she said, putting a scarlet, pointed fingernail on the slender blue line of a river, "that's a gristmill that grinds flour. Folks come from all over to get the stuff, though it's a little rough for my taste. Then there are lumber mills all over."

Faith had the same stunned look that Dana knew was on her own face. A mill had sounded so rare. It hadn't even occurred to her to wonder what kind of mill it might be. She let her breath out slowly, waiting for Faith to respond.

"Well, if you're not particular," Bret said, "we could use the yellow pages."

Dana didn't realize she had spoken the words until she heard her own voice, trembling with doubt.

"But we're particular," she whispered.

"Most of them don't work this time of year anyway," the waitress went on. "It takes a lot of water to keep a mill running with as much cold as we've got. But if you want, I'll give you a list of the ones I know."

Faith was still staring back with that shocked look when the woman moved away. "I didn't think there would be many."

When the waitress came back with a scrawled piece of paper, they took it gratefully and left. She had written the names of the mills and whatever she knew about them.

CHAPTER TWELVE

Waking up was the hardest part of the whole day for Shelley. As she drifted from sleep she was forced to face, even with her eyes closed, the long, cold terror of another day. She delayed this waking as long as she could, pretending, there in the filthy blanket, that she was at home. She tried to reconstruct the comfortable sounds of morning at home. There would be the muted clatter of her mother moving around the kitchen, her father's low rumble as he read the *Des Moines Register*, half to himself and half-aloud to her mother.

The scrape of the door and the thump of her breakfast being set on the stool inside her prison jerked her back to reality.

Huddling in the blanket, she knelt and added another pile of sawdust to her careful record of days. Six piles of sawdust. Six days. She counted on her fingers as she did each

morning. The Sunday she had been kidnapped had been the twenty-first of February. This then, was Saturday the twenty-
seventh.

She rose swiftly, fighting the hot rush of
tears behind her eyes. She had learned a lot
about herself during those days. Crying was
a toboggan ride downhill. If you ever let the
tears start to flow, there would be no stopping
until you crashed with exhaustion, your eyes
swollen and your head aching, throbbing
with pain.

The pitcher of water from the day before
had a slender layer of ice on it. She broke it
and lifted the frail disc of ice out. After
scrubbing at her teeth, she splashed enough
water on her face to take her breath away.
Then, huddled back in her blankets, she
slowly ate the sticky bun and drank the icy
carton of milk.

Six days. She had been in this hateful
place for six whole days. She could pull the
waistband of her skirt out a full inch. Her
hair felt lanky and thick, as if she hadn't
rinsed all the shampoo out. Never in her
life had she gone for six days without a
shower, without washing her hair, without
a change of clothes. And she never would
again.

If only she could go home.

She wished she had some way to write
down all her resolutions. She realized she

was thinking like a child. She even remembered being young enough to try to bribe her mother with promises: "If you let me go, I promise I'll . . . clean my room every day without being told, eat everything on my plate without fussing," and on and on.

There was no way that she could buy her freedom with promises, but she found herself making them anyway. *I'll never go a day without washing my hair. I'll never eat any junk food. I'll never complain about anything. ONLY LET ME GO HOME.*

During the past days, she had learned the rhythm of the small world outside this room. After the quiet of early morning, she often heard the arrival of a car or truck in the yard outside and then the rumble of men's voices.

Sometimes the great saw squealed for a long time, and then there was hammering and an occasional curse. Sometimes a truck horn sounded, and the big door was pushed open. They were selling something, she decided, something they made from the wood they sawed, something small enough to haul away in a car. Then, of course, they also sold great planks, which she heard dragged from a storage room beyond the wall of the little toilet room.

That Saturday morning the sounds started earlier than usual. She heard someone hailing her captors from the road and the big heavy door being pushed open. The men's voices were loud enough that she could hear them without even pressing herself against the wall.

"Snow?" her captor's voice asked. "Don't see any sign of it."

The mumbled response came from farther away as the door was pushed shut. Shelley slumped back on the cot. Snow. The different snows of her life passed through her mind, threatening to start the tears. The snows of Iowa were deep and pure white. Her brothers had rolled great snowmen for her, an army of snowmen taking every knitted hat in the house for their heads. Her mother had complained laughingly that carrot noses were all very good but a few vitamins left in the house wouldn't hurt them either.

Once her father had wakened her at midnight. She must have been about seven. On the fresh glaze of snow she had seen faint, colored lights coming like magic out of the north. He had held her in a blanket while he explained about aurora borealis, the northern lights, and how she must remember because one saw them so rarely.

Snow fell on the grounds of Canby Hall like a benediction. The pine boughs swayed toward the earth, and every sill caught a fluff of white to glisten against the red brick of the fine old buildings.

She didn't know whether it was the threat of snow or just that it was Saturday that brought more business than usual to the mill.

With so many people coming and going, maybe she could scream or give some signal that she was being held a prisoner. The screech of the big saw starting and stopping reminded her that no one could hear her pound or scream over that noise.

There was nothing she could do to help herself. Nothing. By now she was convinced that she had blown the only real chance she would ever get. What had made her think that Faith and Dana would even get to hear what she said to Mr. Flint? She had thought of a dozen better clues she could have given to Casey's father. But her chance was gone, probably forever. The clues she had given him would only be useful to someone who played that silly game that she and her roommates played.

"I Love My Love."

"I love my love with a P because he is precious," she whispered. "His name is Paul . . ." Tears came hot behind her eyes. She got up and walked back and forth across the room twenty times, very fast. As she crossed the last time she saw the first flakes of snow waver past the window.

If she were at home on a Saturday when it was snowing, she and her mother would find something cozy to do. Her mother might read while Shelley made supper. Soup would be nice. Maybe she would make that wonderful Dutch split-pea soup with the little chunks of ham and serve it with homemade French bread with sesame seeds on top.

And if she were at Canby Hall — she gasped aloud. The party. She had forgotten all about the party that she and Faith had planned to give Dana on Monday the twenty-ninth.

Since Dana was a leap-year baby and this was a leap year, she and Faith had planned a perfect four-year-old's party — because at sixteen this would only be Dana's fourth real birthday.

"I can't stand it," she told the quiet room. "I really can't stand it one more minute." Then, after fighting them all day, the tears got away from her. Angry at herself, Shelley jumped up from the cot and went over to the pitcher of water to splash cold water on her face to shock herself back to her senses.

The snow had even worked its way between the cracks of the boards in the primitive little room. She went into the bathroom, where the voices of the men in the storeroom were remarkably clear.

Both men seemed to be in the storeroom. They were apparently moving things around, shoving something this way and that. Their voices sounded cheerful, as if the snow had raised their spirits. But their conversation made no sense to Shelley.

"Well," one of them said brightly. "We're coming up on the first right away. I'll tell you, I'll be darned glad to be free of this hole."

"I've about had it, too," his companion admitted. They shoved something again, and Shelley heard a muffled curse from one of them.

"Be careful, will you?" an angry voice challenged.

"Listen, you're just keyed up. I'm sorry. Like you said, this whole affair is almost over."

"What about her?" the other voice asked. "Do we just walk off and leave her?"

"Why not? He's a big boy. Surely he can follow directions." Then he laughed. "It might take him a day or two, but we can always leave extra food to hold her over."

"Best of all, it worked," the other man said with satisfaction. "It sounded harebrained and dangerous when Ames came up with it, but it worked. The stuff will be safely stashed away, and there's that great law about not being tried twice for the same crime. Without his blabbing, they haven't got a prayer."

"Here, give us a hand with this one," his companion ordered. Then after a minute, he agreed, "A good operation." The scraping stopped, and Shelley heard the heavy door close in the room beyond the wall.

She was freezing. She had stood too long in that miserable little room. With her teeth chattering, she fled to the blanket on the cot. She sat up, Indian fashion, with the blanket peaked up over her head like a hood and tried to figure out what they were talking about.

It was clear enough who "she" was. Her heart sank at the thought of them leaving her here with "extra food."

"*A day or two*." She thought of light coming and fading beyond the window again and again without even the sound of her captors outside the wall.

And what if she weren't found? People had come and gone to the mill all week, but nobody had thought to wonder what was in this room or find any reason to come in here.

"*A big boy who can follow directions*."

Her brother Jeff had a friend at Iowa State who had gone cross-country skiing in the Sierra Nevadas with some people he had just met. There had been an argument of some kind, and the group split up. All of them had made it back to the lodge but Jeff's friend. He had lost his way. Naturally a search was launched. There was even talk of some foul play or that maybe the friend had been injured. That was all just talk. Jeff's friend had lost his way and died of exposure miles from where they first started the search.

She could see the familiar double-draped flags that decorated the top of the *Pine Bluff Adversary*, with the weather report on the left and the current commodity market on the right. Across the middle she saw her own picture. Probably they would run the one from her freshman yearbook from high school, with her hair curled that weird way and her head at a funny angle. The headline was what sent a shiver down her spine: LOCAL GIRL DIES OF EXPOSURE, it read.

She caught herself sharply. From the first, she had decided that there were two hard things she must do. She had kept track of the time all right. Keeping control of her imagination had been harder. Imagining her obituary on the front page of the Pine Bluff paper was not the kind of thinking she should do.

It had grown quiet behind the door, and the light was fading from the snowy window.

She had been through her house back home so many times in her mind that she knew every detail by heart. She had even been through Baker House, trying to remember who lived in every room and even what color spreads they had on the beds.

Paul. She decided to think about Paul. Paul and snow.

She was trying to remember the sleigh ride that Paul's folks had held the year she and Paul were in the eighth grade. She remembered what she had worn, red ski pants with a white jacket and a monster striped scarf that wound around her head a dozen times. She had gotten as far as the huge campfire, with Paul's mother supervising the cooking of the hot dogs, when she drifted off to sleep.

CHAPTER THIRTEEN

The snow began to fall a little before noon. At first it was only a swirling dazzle in the air that whitened the hood of Bret's car but blew away at the smallest spurt of speed.

Halfway through the morning, they had replaced the map torn out of the atlas with a local map that showed every street and lane.

The first false start took them north and a little west of Melrose. When they finally reached the spot that Faith had marked as the exact address of one of the mills, they discovered a used car lot.

"Been gone three years now," the man explained. "It had stood as long as it aimed to, I guess. A big nor'easter blew in and just buckled the walls in, like so many matchsticks. When the man who owned it got it leveled off, he sold the land to this outfit."

"Strike one," Bret pointed out as he thanked the man and drove away.

The Harrison Mill was the next one on Faith's list.

"What does it say about the Harrison Mill?" Bret asked as he started up the road she had marked.

Faith laughed. "It says that old Harrison seems like an ogre but not to pay any mind. 'He has a heart of gold,' " she quoted.

The Harrison mill was shuttered and abandoned. Faith got out and took a few pictures anyway.

Watching from the car, Bret laid his arm across the back of the seat and gently massaged Dana's shoulder under her jacket. "You okay?"

Dana nodded and smiled at him. "You can't imagine what this means to me, Bret. I'm sorry it seems like such a crazy idea, and I do feel bad about wasting your whole Saturday."

"I get to decide when my time is being wasted," he told her, his voice suddenly a little husky. He was embarrassed, Dana realized. "I can't imagine ever thinking any time I spend with you is wasted."

From the corner of her eye, Dana saw Faith picking her way through the brush to return to the car. Leaning over, Dana pressed a quick kiss on Bret's cheek. He turned to her, startled. If Faith had not been right at the door, she knew he wouldn't have settled for a peck on the cheek the second time.

"You kiddies staying warm enough?" Faith asked brightly. "There's a sign on the mill door that says, "ESTATE SALE.""

"Ah," Dana said. "Mr. Harrison must have died."

"Even hearts of gold eventually stop," Bret said, backing out to return to the main road.

The silence from the backseat was deeper than an ordinary quiet. Dana waited a moment before turning to Faith.

"Quick, before our umpire here calls that as a second strike, do you have another mill on that list?"

"Only one." Faith's tone was subdued. She passed Dana the map, pointing to a penciled line with a slender finger. "Maybe we should give up on that one. It says it is a flour mill and the pond sometimes freezes."

"Even the worst batter deserves three strikes," Bret pointed out. "The day is still young."

As it turned out, Faith's suggestion had been inspired. The pond at the next mill was indeed frozen. A typed notice inside the glass door that led to the office invited the reader to "COME BACK IN THE SPRING." Underneath was a handwritten note: "STONE GROUND WHEAT AND CORN. SINCE 1853."

The dazzle of snow had become definable flakes spinning in the still air. The movement of the windshield wipers created twin fans that opened from whiteness into whiteness.

Faith was getting quieter and quieter back in the seat behind them. Dana knew she was wondering what wild goose chase she had brought them on. More to encourage Faith than for any other reason, she said, "You said yourself the day was young."

"Maybe we could stop for lunch and regroup," Bret suggested. "The road is all I seem to be able to handle. Why don't you two watch for a lunch place?"

Dana always thought of Greenleaf as being the country. This area made that village look like a metropolis. They passed a town and saw no cars along the street. The only light was inside the back of a gas station.

"This is a ghost town," Faith decided. "Who ever heard of a ghost town in Massachusetts?"

"Maybe everybody with any sense has gone home," Bret suggested. "This is getting to be snow on snow around here."

"It's just that it's Saturday," Dana countered. "Maybe they don't like to come out on Saturday."

Bret laughed at her logic but drove on. Within a mile they saw a roadside café with lights at the windows.

A single car was buried in the parking lot outside the kitchen door. As Bret pulled into the lot, his horn began to blare. He was slapping the wheel desperately when an old man in a greasy apron opened the door and glared out at him.

"There's no curb service here," he shouted. "Just come on in or forget it."

"The horn's stuck," Bret yelled back.

"Can't hear you." The old man shook his head. Dana got out and started for the door.

"His horn is stuck," she told the man.

"Oh." The old man nodded. In a cramped, uneven walk, he came down the stairs and gave Bret's car a swift kick on the right front fender.

The sound stopped instantly.

"You folks hungry?" the old man asked, as if he did this service every day.

"Well, yes," Bret admitted.

"Decide fast," the old man said, pulling up his sweater and starting for the door again. "I should be shutting up to go home, but there's still some chowder left."

"Chowder," Dana echoed, realizing how many miles they had covered since her scrambled eggs and toast.

"Wipe your feet there," the old man said, preceding them into his restaurant.

You could smell the chowder from the door. There were only about five tables in the room, and each one was covered with a plastic cloth decorated with daisies. A tray of condiments, mustard, catsup, and so forth, served as centerpieces, but the air was rich with a good clam aroma.

"Hate to throw the stuff out," the old man said, as he set steaming bowls on the tables. "Especially if I could sell it. This might be a holiday snow, you know."

"Holiday snow?" Bret asked.

He nodded. "If the plows don't start right away on this, there'll be no going nowhere. That makes it a holiday."

"There will be plows," Bret said hopefully.

"Sometimes, sometimes not, on state roads," the old man said. "Want white bread or brown?"

Dana had been thinking of crackers, but the broad loaves of homemade bread that he set on the wooden board were irresistible.

Dana realized the old man was lonesome. After refilling Bret's bowl, he perched on a chair at the next table, chattering as if he had known them forever. "I don't recall seeing you kids in these parts," he suggested. "You from away?"

"Down by Greenleaf," Dana told him, buttering another slice of the marvelous bread.

"Greenleaf, eh?" He rose and tottered away to return with a canning jar half-full of jam.

"Try this on that bread," he suggested. "It's fifty cents extra but worth it. My wife puts it up from those little plums out at Grangers. You know Grangers?"

"We don't really know anyone," Bret told him. "We came up here looking for a mill around Melrose."

The old man laughed. "You came about a

dozen years too late, son. There used to be mills along these rivers that you couldn't count, but that's all over now."

With a sinking heart, Dana was watching the thickening snow beyond the window. How could she ask Bret to follow any more leads when even an old man like this couldn't come up with a mill?

"But no mills working now?" Bret pressed hopefully.

"Not as I can think of," the old man said. "There's about one more bowl of that chowder left in the pot. You can have it for free."

Bret finished the last bowl with a groan. "Well" — he looked hopefully from Dana to Faith — "if there aren't any more mills . . ."

Dana was counting out the money for the lunch. The old man cackled and grinned at Bret. "I was wrong," he told him. "You weren't born ten years too late — I was. No good-looking girl ever offered to buy *my* lunch."

"He's earned it in this mill search." Dana smiled, adding a tip.

He loaded a tray with their plates as they put on their jackets. They were at the door when he set the tray down with a clatter. "I tell you, the years are getting to me. It just come to me what mill you want. It's that lumber mill up on the creek yonder. It keeps going, I tell you, and will forever. Well, at least as long as those hurricanes rip along this coast. Folks need lumber to fasten their places up, and the man who owns it is the last man around here who can build a box worth shipping things in."

Dana turned to him eagerly, ignoring Bret's groan.

"Is it far?" she asked.

"Not as the crow flies," he said. "By roads it's maybe ten miles or so."

"Or so," Bret echoed under his breath.

"Now don't behave like that," the old man rebuked him. "After she bought you that chowder and all."

Faith giggled softly as she unfolded the map on the table. "Can you show us how to get from here to there?" she asked.

"No problem," he said, wetting the lead of his pencil before he began to write. "Right up here, to the intersection and swing a right," he began.

"How are the roads?" Bret asked.

"Good roads most of the way," he replied, nodding as he drew the wavering line along the map. "There's a stretch of maybe a mile of heavy going right at the last, but you could walk in for that. No distance at all. You'll see the mill up among the trees. Big place. The family that built it lived there. It's got a lot of little rooms and a green roof that shows through the trees from the road."

"Good hunting," he called after them, watching from the door as they started down to the car.

"Listen, you all," Bret began when the windshield wipers swept the mounds of snow back from the glass. "Don't you really think . . ."

"I really think we have to try just this one," Faith broke in. "If this is not the right place, we give up and start home — no argument. He said there would be snowplows."

Bret sighed and shifted the car into reverse. It complained and skidded a little in its tracks. On the third try he broke through the snow piled against the tires.

"I promise," Dana told him. "If this isn't it, we give up and go straight back home."

"I have a witness," he said, trying to keep his voice calm as he slid the car from the parking lot into the snow-packed street.

CHAPTER FOURTEEN

The storm had settled in. They had wasted too much time looking for an open restaurant. In honesty, Dana didn't begrudge the time they had spent with the old man. There had always been the chance that the snow would stop. It definitely hadn't.

Although it was only a little after three in the afternoon, Bret turned on the headlights. They didn't help very much, only making a twin tunnel of lights through which the broad, flat flakes fell steadily. The traffic was totally gone from the streets. Behind the snow-covered trees, lights winked from warm houses. The air was fragrant with wood smoke.

Then the houses were farther apart, and Bret peered intently, slowing down until he was barely creeping along the country lane.

Suddenly Faith, in the backseat, gave a shriek. A huge German shepherd was running alongside the car, barking furiously and lunging at the window.

"We won't hurt him, will we?" she asked when she caught her breath.

Bret's brief laugh was not humorous. "At four miles an hour?" he asked, still straining to see the road ahead.

As suddenly as he had come, the dog retreated to post himself on a bank by the side of the road and bark furiously after them. His coat was so matted with snow that only his eyes and mouth showed color.

"Ran out of his own territory," Dana guessed aloud.

"That makes two of us," Bret murmured. "Madness, absolute madness."

"This is the very last one we'll try to find," Dana reminded him. "The very last, final one."

It might as well have been completely dark for all the visibility outside. Dana groaned inwardly to think of the faith they were putting in the penciled directions Faith had scribbled on her lunch napkin. She was very conscious of Bret's skill in keeping the car on the road. The turns were particularly bad. The station wagon fishtailed, waggling them from side to side, so that Bret fought for his hold on the wheel. At one left turn the horn began again, blaring into the silence.

"Want to stop?" Faith asked. "I studied his kicking technique. I'm sure I could do as well."

Bret shook his head. "Thanks, Faith, but you might have to push us to start again. Sometimes it stops by itself."

Then as a truck approached, coming from the other direction, Bret clung to his side of the road with nervous care. "The horn may actually be a safety factor, for all I know. Even if they don't see my lights, they can sure hear me coming."

The next turn was onto a bigger road. The horn stopped as suddenly as it had begun.

"We're almost there," Dana said excitedly.

"This is where we should start watching. The lane, as the old man called it, goes off this road," Faith said.

This was clearly a major road. Two full lanes ran in each direction. Bret picked up speed.

"Hey, this has been plowed," he decided aloud. "The storm is staying ahead of it, but at least a plow has been over it once."

"Slow down," Faith called from the backseat. "We're supposed to be able to see the green roof of the mill above those trees along here."

"All I see above the trees is more snow coming," Dana admitted. "And more snow and more snow."

As Bret drove around the long sweep of a curve, Dana felt something catch in her chest. "That's it," she cried. "I see it, look there to the left. A green roof just like he said!"

The lane led through the woods toward the mill, whose green roof peaked solidly among the feathery, snowcapped trees. A wisp of smoke trailed upward into the snowy air. The trees along the lane would have hidden a light if there had been one, but the pillar of smoke battling through the falling snow was assurance that someone was there.

"Help me make the turn," Bret ordered.

With the window rolled down, the snowflakes fell cool and delicious against Dana's face as she directed Bret on the turn. The passing of the snowplow had left a ridge at the end of the lane. At first the car balked. Only after several tries did Bret force it over the obstacle to shudder onto the deep snow of the road.

"Any idea how far we have to go to reach that place?" Bret asked, his voice hesitant.

"Not really," Faith told him. "He only said it was a little ways up there."

Bret had shifted down to fight both the snowy road and the upward grade.

"If you think we can possibly walk it, we'll have a better chance of getting out of here later," Bret suggested. "In fact, if we can turn around, that would be the thing to do right now. It's always nice to have a little gravity on your side."

Bret battled the car forward only a few more yards before the trail widened. It took three tries, but Bret was finally able to turn the car around so that it faced the road. He killed the engine with a sigh and turned to grin at Dana.

"Remember?" he asked. "I'm the guy who signed up to take driver's ed in the spring because I hated winter driving." He squeezed Dana's hand. "Don't tell me what I'm doing here because I wouldn't believe any story you gave me."

As he had done when they approached the abandoned Harrison Mill and again when they found the flour mill with the frozen pond, Bret frowned and said something about "weird" or "spooky."

This time Dana knew very well what he meant. Through the thick snow-covered trees all they could see of the mill was that green roof and the fingering plume of smoke. Dana felt herself shiver there in the warm car as she stared toward the place.

Once the motor was silenced, the woods seemed to speak in a restless voice of its own. Now and then they heard the crack of a limb. Off somewhere, a dog howled mournfully, as if expecting no answer.

And steadily, like an eerie sound from another season, came the sound of falling water, a slow, almost musical background to the forest sounds.

Between them, Dana and Faith had agreed that the most unsuspicious way to approach a stranger was with an obvious camera slung over your shoulder. Everyone always seemed anxious to help a young photographer accumulate shots.

"How convincing is this camera going to be here?" Faith asked quietly from the backseat.

Dana looked around at her, horrified.

Faith grinned and shrugged. "Well, maybe I didn't hear the weather report."

Bret was looking from one to the other of them and frowning. Dana was glad he knew that they were covertly looking for Shelley. If she had not told him, she would have more explaining to do now than she was ready to tackle.

"It doesn't look as if any of us heard a weather report," Bret said brightly. "Let's go if we're going to go."

Dana shook her head. "You stay with the car."

"Well." Faith seemed to be trying to frame some instinct into words. "If it's the right place, maybe . . ." she suggested. Her eyes were luminous on Dana. "Nobody's going to believe this camera no matter what I say. It's snowed almost all day. Sooner or later they're going to notice us through the trees," Faith said. She slid her camera over the sleeve of her down jacket. "Off I go." Her tone was obviously meant to sound hearty. It failed.

"'Off I go'?" Dana echoed. "Don't you want me to come along like before?"

Faith shook her head. "For some reason I'm wary of us both going at once. Maybe we could break up."

"How about having a car stuck in the snow?" Bret suggested. Then he tightened his shoulders with a groan. "I haven't a pig's idea of what's going on. What is everybody suddenly so tense about?"

Dana pulled on her mittens and opened the door. "Nothing," she lied. "Faith and I are going to go up there separately and look around."

"I can come along," Bret offered.

Dana shook her head. "If you want to get to a spot where you could watch us, that might be useful."

They were parked closer to the mill than Dana realized. As she rounded the bend, sinking now and then in the snow-filled ruts, the building practically loomed above her. With a discreet, reassuring wave back to Faith, she studied the scene.

The mill building stood to her left, a huge square shaft of wood with high windows up near the roof. The sound of the waterfall was suddenly much louder, although she couldn't see it. The big, ugly mill building obscured the waterfall from her view, but she saw the dark flow of the stream wending toward it from farther up the hill.

The building stood in an untidy lot. Piles of lumber were stacked here and there, all neatly capped by the fresh snow. A flatbed truck loaded with more planks and boards was near a van. Dana could see no way to enter the building from this direction. She stood listening in the shadows of the trees a long time before venturing across the open space to get closer to the building.

She was out in the clearing when a sudden burst of sound stopped her heart in her throat. A heavy door scraped. Men's voices sounded loud and near. She would have fled, but there wasn't time. They came around the corner of the building, bearing a large wooden crate between them. "Easy," she heard one man say. "Watch your step."

When they saw her, they came to an instant stop.

"Hey, you," one of the men shouted. He might have dropped his corner of the crate except for his companion's warning.

"Quick now," the other man said, "down easy."

Later she realized that if she had just stood there, spoken quietly, and explained about the car being stuck, a lot of later trouble would have been avoided. Instead, she stared at the crate they were carrying with horror.

These were not just any wooden boxes. The crate the men were carrying was only a larger version of those distinctive crates that Casey Flint used for storage, exactly like the one she and Faith had carried up to the penthouse with Casey's clothes in it.

She must have shown her horror in her face, for the larger of the two men started toward her.

She didn't even have sense enough to run for the car. She bent into the wind and started around the building away from them. They were shouting for her to stop, to come back.

She was too terrified even to think. She recognized one of the men instantly. Even with a knitted hat hooding his forehead she knew that face. This was the man Faith had photographed, standing among the crowd at Canby Hall on Parent-Alumnae Weekend. This was the man in the beret leaning against the pier, watching Mr. Flint in Casey's picture.

"How did she get in here?" one of the men shouted. "You go check the road."

There was no time to stop to get her bearings. There wasn't even time to watch out for her footing. Leaning into the storm, Dana ran along the path that lay between the mill pond and the mill itself. The giant wheel was still turning slowly, dripping ice water back into the pond. A fine spray had glazed the path with ice. The man was shouting and gaining on her as she tried to swerve away from that strip of ice.

She felt her foot miss the solid path and tried to hurl her weight back toward safety. Instead she tumbled head over heels and gasped as the water of the mill pond covered her. She surfaced, thrashing desperately. The chill seemed to penetrate her bones.

"You can't have lost her," the other man said, joining her pursuer. "She's got to be in the pond."

She heard his brief laugh. "Then she's no problem. She won't last long there, not in this weather."

As she heard the crunch of his feet nearing, she filled her lungs with breath and submerged. Underwater, she worked her way toward the outcropping that had given way under her weight.

He was right, of course. No one, even dressed as she was in heavy thermal gear, could last long in that water. She heard them hesitate above her.

"So if she's alone, it's okay," one man said reasonably. "If she isn't, we'd better get a move on."

"You watch here," his companion said. "I'll finish loading."

She came up for air, smelled cigarette smoke, and heard the scrape of the door again. Then a voice called crossly from farther away. "I need help with this big one. There's only one more. Any sign of her?"

"By now she's a goner," his companion said. "Or nearly so. What does it take to freeze somebody? Three or four minutes, isn't it?"

Dana felt the chill moving in along her veins. She waggled her feet desperately and moved her shoulders up and down. Three or four minutes. Already her hands were numb and tears she didn't know she was shedding froze on her cheeks.

Three or four minutes.

CHAPTER FIFTEEN

When they left the car, Dana had made her way north to the mill. Faith had gone south through the trees. From where Faith stood in the shadows of the trees, she could see the mill and the pond. There had to be someone in there, with that smoke trailing upward and the van and truck parked so casually in the open lot. By shifting a little, Faith got an angled view of the door of the mill. It was a big door, obviously designed to permit large objects to pass in and out. She wished she could see the roof better. If people were living there or keeping a kidnapped girl prisoner, there should be extra pipes to vent the stove and the plumbing. From this angle only a rude chimney was visible on the green roof.

Within minutes she realized that Dana had trapped herself by choosing the direction she did. The only way Dana could get near the building was to pass over a large open space. Even if she were not seen as she passed, her footsteps on that untouched blanket of snow would be a dead giveaway that someone was prowling around.

Until this moment Faith hadn't really admitted to herself that she might have dragged Dana and Bret into a deadly adventure. There was so much to lose. Even if they survived this, if she and Dana were shown to have checked out of Baker illegally, they would both be expelled. As for Bret — she wondered how Oakley Prep would react to his having sheltered two runaway girls in the parking lot. There had to be at least as many rules for the Oakley Prep boys as there were for the Canby Hall girls.

But she had needed to help so badly. The rising panic of the past week must have fuzzed up her mind. In spite of all her life experience, she had let herself believe that she and Dana could rescue Shelley by the sheer force of love.

This wasn't the first time she had let her imagination run away from her. She shivered in the shadows of the trees, remembering.

She had done the same thing when she lost her father.

Faith just wouldn't let herself believe her father was dead. She had made up a dozen stories that she told herself in the quiet of her bed.

Her daddy was off on a secret mission, and they had to give out that story.

Someone else had been mistaken for Danny Thompson in an identical blue uniform.

He was hurt, she would allow that, but when he was better, he would come home again like always.

Of course, that had all been in her head. You can't bring anyone back by love alone. Had she twisted this hope of hers into clues and dragged Dana and Bret into trouble with her?

She watched Dana struggle with the uneven footing of the snowy road. Just as Dana started across the clearing past the truck and the van, Faith saw what Dana couldn't see. She saw a wide fan of light glaze the snow as the big door swung open.

Two men were framed against the light. They leaned to lift something from the floor. From that distance Faith could only see that it was some sort of wooden box. She guessed it was heavy from the way the men handled themselves.

Faith groaned. Now Dana would tell them about car trouble. They would probably go down the road to help Bret out. They would have no excuse to get into the mill to see if Shelley were hidden there. They had come all this way and taken all these risks for nothing.

Faith watched as the men maneuvered their burden down the steps and onto the path that led along the side of the stream. They cleared the corner of the mill on their way to the parking area before either of them saw Dana. They stopped dead at the sight of her in the middle of the clearing.

Faith sighed. Once Dana talked to them about the car trouble, the whole trip would be wasted.

But no. They wouldn't have seen *her*. The minute they started off down the road toward Bret's car, *she* could search the mill for Shelley. Even at the thought, she felt her heart begin to pump faster and realized her mouth was suddenly dry.

Moving very slowly, Faith drew closer to the tree beside her. Even as she positioned herself, she realized that something was wrong, terribly wrong.

Instead of replying to the man's call, Dana had seemed to freeze in place for a long minute. Then, without a word that Faith could hear, Dana wheeled and began to run around the mill as rapidly as she could on the rough, snowy earth.

The men had laid down their burden. One followed her in a great loping run as she disappeared behind the far side of the mill.

Before Faith could even think of what to do, she heard the distant shouts of the man and a scream, a girl's scream. Then silence.

Something had to have scared Dana very badly to send her running like that — and in the wrong direction. Bret. The only thing Faith could do was to get help. Trying to keep herself low behind the shrubby trees that thickened the woods, she made her way back to the car.

Bret had heard Dana's scream. He was climbing out of the car as Faith neared him.

Awkward with haste, he slid as he stepped out and fell heavily against the side of the car.

The silence of the woods was fractured by a sudden blast of sound. That ridiculous horn was stuck again.

"Go," Faith shouted at him. "Start the motor and go."

He stared at her dumbly, hesitating.

"Go, Bret," she pleaded. "Dana needs help."

She could hear the men in the clearing behind her shouting in confusion. But where was Dana?

Leaving Bret, Faith worked her way back through the trees. She was too far to hear their conversation, but the men were loading the crates onto the van almost desperately. With the last of the crates inside, she saw the taller man, the one who had chased Dana, stretch and pull a gun from his pocket to start down the road toward the sound of Bret's blasting horn.

Bret obeyed her plea. The motor roared even above the honking of the horn as he jockeyed the car desperately to get it started down the hill.

The running man passed within inches of her, his face tight with fury. Faith ached for a weapon, any weapon to stop his race toward Bret. He was only a car's length behind Bret when the station wagon broke free to hurtle down the lane toward the road, throwing a fan of icy snow and slush back on Bret's pursuer.

Dana, Faith's mind kept repeating, *where is Dana?*

Even as she glued herself against the tree, the men were shouting at each other. The honking of Bret's horn was fading in the distance. *He'll find help,* Faith promised herself, trying to remember the last sign of life they had seen before the turnoff.

"Get a move on," the man in the van was shouting. "We're pulling out."

"What about the girl?" the man with the gun shouted back.

"You'll have to help me with her," his companion replied. "We can't leave her here now."

When they both disappeared into the mill, Faith raced through the trees, careless of cover. She was close enough to the truck to crouch behind it when they came out from behind the mill again. Clearly, it took all of their combined strength to hold the blanketed figure fighting in their arms. After thrusting their victim into the back of the van, they both leaped in and backed up swiftly, their snow tires leaving deep ridges in the ground.

Faith watched them pass with helpless tears streaming down her face. They would catch up with Bret within a mile. The van was powerful and equipped with special tires.

There was no point in crying. It was over. They had lost. They had not only lost Shelley, but Dana, too. Who knew what they would do when they overtook Bret?

She wasn't really crying now. It was just that helpless tears coursed hot and painful down her icy face. They had left the light on in the mill. It streamed golden on the snow. Faith stared at it numbly.

A phone. They must have a phone in the mill.

Faith worked her way swiftly along the side of the building toward the open door. A single bare bulb hung from the ceiling. Beneath the light stood a table with its chair knocked over onto the floor. Faith found the phone near the outside door and dialed.

"Kidnap," she gasped when the operator came on. "An old lumber mill." Why couldn't she remember the name of the mill? Or even the last town they had been through? But she did remember the name of the road they had turned off from. The operator hung up, cautioning her to stay by the phone after taking the number.

Faith stared about at the great shadowy room with its windows plastered with snow. Old lumber was everywhere along three of the walls. On the fourth there was a primitive sink. Crowded on its drainboard were a tin coffeepot and some grocery bags. Two cots lined the wall. At the other end of the room, a door stood ajar.

The sound of the waterfall bothered her. If only it were quieter. If only the operator would call to tell her the van had been caught.

She walked to the door of the room and looked in. A filthy cot stood on a bedding of stale sawdust. Aside from the cot there was only a rough bench with a pitcher and a bowl on it.

A closet-sized room in one corner held a toilet with a gravity tank set above it. She was turning to go back to the phone when she saw a touch of color in the sawdust.

She knelt to pick it up and felt her knees almost buckle. *Shelley*.

It was a plastic barrette in the shape of a tied bow. It was that dreadful orange color that Shelley insisted on wearing even though it clashed with her blond hair. Faith remembered seeing that barrette the day of the Parent-Alumnae dinner. Shelley had worn it in her hair as she leaned to talk to Casey's Aunt Edie.

Faith felt herself suddenly without strength. She couldn't even lift herself from the kneeling position. She only held the barrette in her hand and stared at it. They had been right. Shelley had been here once. The clues had been real. Shelley had done all she could do to save herself, but they had come too late.

The phone began to peal in the next room. Faith dragged herself to her feet with a sick feeling of despair.

The moment she spoke, a man's voice interrupted her crisply. "Only one question," he asked. "Would the car and the van be going north or south along the highway from the mill?"

"South," Faith mumbled. He hung up at once. She stood a moment staring dumbly at the phone, the barrette still tight in her hand.

When she first heard the sound she told herself she was imagining it. Tightening her shoulders, she forced herself to turn. Someone was at the open doorway, trying to crawl in. The sound she had heard was a kind of a gasping.

"Help," the voice rasped. "Please help me. I'm freezing."

As she spoke, Dana's head drooped. She would have fallen back through the open doorway if Faith had not been there instantly at her side, catching her weight and tugging her inside.

CHAPTER SIXTEEN

Dana was well past giving Faith any help at all. Just getting her friend hauled over the doorsill and into the room turned into a major project. Dana, who usually seemed all slender grace, had become a great sodden mass that prickled with elbows and knees. It was almost as if Dana were half-asleep. She kept trying to talk, only to have her words trail off into helpless tears.

When Faith had finally managed to half drag, half carry Dana into the warm room, she looked around desperately.

How could she know so much and all of the wrong things? She knew how to stop bleeding with a tourniquet, and brace a broken bone. She had even mastered the Heimlich Maneuver, which kept a person from choking, or thought she had. Mouth-to-mouth resuscitation had been the easiest thing she had learned in the whole lifesaving course her mother had talked her into taking. If she had learned anything about handling a half-frozen person, the limp figure of Dana shivering inside the door had driven it from her mind.

Heat, Faith decided. Dana had to be warmed up, inside and out, as quickly as possible.

After filling the old tin coffeepot with water, Faith turned the electric plate all the way up. All the heat in the room was coming from a small black metal stove, whose dusty pipe angled toward the high ceiling. Kneeling, Faith opened the little round door. A blast of warm air hit her and the glow of red shown from the ashes. The only pieces of wood in the rusty bucket looked too big to coax a flame from those coals. She threw in the smallest of them hopefully and turned back to Dana.

The color of Dana's face and hands frightened Faith. Her nose and cheeks, which had been a flaming red, had lost their glow and faded to a sickly pallor. She had to get Dana out of those icy wet clothes even if there was nothing to wrap her in except the filthy blanket from one of the cots against the wall.

When a faint crackling began in the belly of the stove, Faith led Dana close to it. Then it was like trying to undress a large, shivering doll. Dana seemed only half-conscious of what Faith was trying to do. As Faith struggled to get her friend's arms out of the sodden jacket and sweater, Dana rubbed at her nose and cheeks with the back of her hands and whimpered like a puppy.

Only when her wet clothes were off and Dana was curled in the blanket by the stove's increasing warmth, did the coffeepot begin to steam. Since Faith found no tea among the clutter of grocery items by the sink, she rinsed an earthenware mug and filled it with steaming water.

"Try to drink this," she coaxed Dana. "Get it down as hot as you can." Dana could barely manage to hold the mug without spilling the blazing water down her front. She hardly drank any of it, but Faith decided that holding the steaming cup before her frozen face had to be better than nothing.

"Keep drinking that," Faith ordered. "I'll find something for you to put on."

"Something" turned out to be a pair of worn and faded overalls and a green, hooded sweatshirt with the kangaroo pocket half torn off.

"Never mind," Faith teased Dana, as she made a belt around the sweatshirt with a soiled rope. "You could start a new bulky style with these."

Dana's shivering seemed to be lessening. She raised her eyes to Faith over the rim of the mug. "The pond," she explained through chattering teeth. "I fell in the pond . . . and Faith, that man . . ."

"Never mind the man," Faith said. "Try to drink that hot water and give me your other hand."

Maybe Faith imagined the warmth coming back into Dana's hand as she rubbed it between her own. Dana seemed to be getting drowsy again, her eyes half-lidded in that pale face. "The man," she repeated, "the man in the pictures you had. And the crates."

"You ran," Faith reminded her. "And he chased you."

Faith couldn't meet Dana's eyes. She was painfully conscious of the curve of the orange barrette in her jeans' pocket. After all this, how could she tell Dana that they had failed? The memory of the men fighting the kicking bundle into the van made her a little sick. Where was Shelley now?

"Bret," Dana remembered.

"He went for help." Faith glanced at the phone. Maybe she should call again. Maybe she should call for an ambulance or something. Dana seemed to weave between limp exhaustion and terrified anxiety.

The only stockings Faith could find had clearly already been worn. They had been abandoned in a heap in the corner of the room. They were dirty and huge but were made of good, solid scratchy wool.

The night was black beyond the window and the last of the wood crackled in the little black stove. Dana's eyes widened.

"Voices," she whispered urgently. "Oh, Faith, he's coming back, hide me."

Faith rose and went to the door. Dana was right. Faith heard not only men's voices shouting, but the sudden scrape of a footstep on the platform outside the door.

"Don't let them in," Dana whimpered. "Don't let them in."

But Faith, there by the door, felt herself grow suddenly weak with relief. The voice was Bret's, and he was calling her name and pounding on the wooden door. "Faith, Faith, are you in there?" he called urgently.

"Bret," she cried, throwing her weight against the heavy door to push it open.

Bret, framed against the snowy woods, was the most beautiful sight she had seen in her life. And beyond him, down the road, she saw lights, colored lights, the whirling blue and red of a police car and uniformed men running toward the mill through the snowy woods.

Without even understanding why they were there or how Bret had managed to return to the mill, Faith fell in his arms.

"Oh, Bret, Bret," she cried. "They didn't catch you. They had a gun."

He didn't reply. She felt him stiffen in her arms as he looked past her. Pulling back, she realized that he was staring at Dana as if in disbelief.

"Dana," he whispered. Then his voice

caught with a tone of jubilation. He was past
Faith and at Dana's side in a few swift steps.
He knelt beside her and seized her by the
arms.

"You're alive, Oh, Dana."

Dana stared at Faith in confusion as Bret
dropped his head against Dana's chest and
held her tight. Dana set down the mug and
patted him like a child. "Bret," she said softly,
"I'm all right, I really am."

Bret's face shone with happiness as he
turned to Faith. "They said she was dead,
drowned in the mill pond."

"They?" Faith asked.

Bret had no chance to answer her question. The room seemed suddenly full of uniformed men. One had a walkie-talkie and
was reporting crisply into it.

"Both here, both seemingly okay. That's
right . . . both." He turned to Dana and
grinned. "I guess you're Dana Morrison, the
one who was supposed to have drowned in
the pond?"

Dana nodded.

"And you must be Faith Thompson?"

At Faith's nod, he returned to his speaker.
"Can you get a vehicle up closer to the place?
Not an ambulance, but I'd hate to see the
Morrison girl try to walk very far."

"Never mind that," Bret put in quickly.
"We can carry her."

That was Dana's first smile.

"Don't kid yourself, lady," Bret told her. "We might slip and slide a little."

The policeman grinned at her. "This snow isn't letting up and the car doesn't have four-wheel drive. I could probably take over if your friend here weakens."

The policeman who accompanied Bret and Dana down the snowy road toward the car took Dana's sodden clothes along in a rough wooden crate. The second policeman stayed behind to put out the fire and secure the mill. "There's been enough excitement around here without a three-alarm fire," he told them.

Faith hung back until Bret and Dana were out of earshot.

"Thanks so much for coming so fast," she told him. "I realized after I called that I wasn't much help in giving directions."

He was pouring water onto her carefully nurtured fire. He looked up at her in amazement. "I didn't come for any call. We were just patrolling. Lots of drivers can't handle this much snow. We always stay close to the plows to try to prevent accidents." He chuckled as he turned back to the fire. "It usually works, too. Not every time, but usually."

After a last glance around, he shut the heavy door and nodded. "Let's try to catch up with that pair. I need to be back on my radio."

The radio certainly wasn't waiting for him.

They could hear its clamor from several yards away. Dana was already in the car as the policeman was trying to turn it around in the deep snow, with the help of Bret's shoulder pushing for dear life.

"Jump in there," the policeman told Faith. "I'll give your friend a hand here."

Faith slid in by Dana and took her hand. Her hand was warm again, warm and soft, feeling like Dana's hand was supposed to feel.

"I'm so happy," Dana whispered. "We made it. Thanks to Bret, we made it."

Faith only nodded. Had Dana forgotten about Shelley? Dana started to speak again, only to be drowned out by the sudden jerking forward of the car and the driver shouting.

"Run alongside and jump in," he called to Bret and his companion. "I don't want to risk stopping again."

It seemed that they were no sooner all crowded into the car than they rolled around the last curve and could see the major road up ahead.

Faith sat up straight in disbelief. This was a madhouse. There seemed to be patrol cars everywhere. The brilliant beam of a snowplow spun in the falling snow a few yards away.

"What's all this?" she cried.

"Ask your friend there," the driver chuckled. "It was almost entirely his party."

CHAPTER SEVENTEEN

Faith was still trying to sort the scene out when the driver pulled to a stop at the side of the road.

Dana had the door open and was out in the snow in a second. She was fighting her baggy clothes and dragging the dirty blanket behind her. Bret had pulled his stocking cap over her head before he carried her out of the mill. If Faith hadn't been so concerned about her and so confused, she would have laughed out loud. What would Dana's fashion-conscious New York mother think if she could see her wading in stocking feet through the snow in that getup?

Dana knocked all thought out of Faith with her shouted question. "Where is she?" Dana called, looking around excitedly. "Where is Shelley?"

Faith's heart dropped. What was Dana

thinking of? Faith could only see the struggling body being thrown into the back of the van.

Bret had piled out of the other side of the police car. The officer at the wheel turned to grin at Faith. "Your friend moves pretty well for a drowned person, doesn't she?"

Before Faith could respond, someone jumped out of one of the police cars blocking the road. With a cry, she flew into Dana's open arms.

Shelley. Faith leaned back weakly against the seat and felt hot tears on her face. *I don't even have to understand,* she told herself aloud. *Thank God. Thank God.*

Bret leaned back into the car and said, "Great, isn't it?" Then he added ruefully, "But you could have told me, you know. When a guy is going out on this kind of errand, he wants to be dressed for it. Did you think I didn't have any shining armor or something? I could have gone to Rent-A-Lance or something."

Then, seeing Faith's face, he slid back in beside her. "Faith! You didn't know, did you? You didn't know that Shelley was down here safe and sound. I had a chance to tell Dana as we came down to the car. Shelley's fine. She's even better than usual — if you share my taste for girls on the skinny side."

"But how, Bret?" Faith asked. "How did it all happen?"

He pulled her from the car. "Come and have a look."

As they passed the two parked police cars, Faith let out a gasp of amazement. Some of the confusion of the colored lights was from a tow-truck, trying to remove Bret's station wagon from the upraised blade of a snowplow.

"Bret," she cried. "What happened?"

Before he could answer, Shelley had grabbed her in a giant hug and was crying against Faith's cheek. She didn't say anything but "Oh, oh, oh," over and over.

That was enough. She held Shelley tight and grinned over her shoulder at Dana. "We love our love with an S," she whispered.

They had done it. Maybe someday, somehow, she would understand how it had all come about. For now it was enough to have the three of them all together in that brightly lit, snowy road with Shelley murmuring, "Oh, oh, oh."

Later Faith always had trouble remembering the name of that little country town where they all ended up. She would, however, never forget the warmth of that off-duty room in the police station. The air of the room was rich with the scent of coffee, but there was also a kettle that was heated again and again for steaming mugs of tea.

The sheriff's wife sent over a box full of sandwiches. They were made on homemade bread spread thickly with butter. There was almost more sliced roasted chicken in hers than Faith could get her mouth around. The chicken tasted like home, faintly perfumed with sage and onion as if it had been bursting with stuffing at least once in its history. The sheriff's wife sent an apology that she didn't have a whole cake, but the applesauce cake she sent made ample slices for all around. The extra slice went to Shelley, who, as Bret had said, was anything but the well-rounded girl they had last seen the Sunday before.

Little by little, Faith got the whole story from the roomful of excited talkers.

"I was up there about twenty yards ahead of the plow when I heard this honking and looked around," one of the policemen explained. "Here was this crazy guy in a station wagon barreling down that mill road at white heat. He hit the ridge left at the entrance of the mill road and stuck up on it like a bug on a pin. He gunned that car and rocked a minute before coming off that ridge like a shot, his horn still blaring. I knew he was in trouble the minute he hit the road. He was spinning out of control every which way, and these plows don't stop on any dime, you know."

"I was totally out of control," Bret admitted. "I didn't even have time to think about it. I knew I didn't dare hit my brake, but there was this *thing* coming at me, spitting snow in all directions."

"What did you do?" Dana asked, leaning over so that the tassel of Bret's stocking cap swung over her cheek.

Bret leaned and flipped it back over her shoulder with a grin. "I suppose it was a creditable performance. I did a couple of fast loops before using the blade of the snowplow as a brake." He grinned. "It's funnier now than it was then, and I have a feeling it's also funnier now than it will be later."

"He made us one great roadblock," the officer put in.

"And it stopped the horn from blowing," Bret added. "It worked just as good as kicking it."

"But the van," Faith asked. "The last I saw, you had been stuffed into that van."

Shelley nodded. "Screaming my head off, I might add. They didn't even take the time to tie me up. The van came out of the mill road just a few seconds after Bret did. The police had stopped on the north, and the snowplow was all tangled with Bret's car on the south. Maybe if they had stopped, or if I hadn't been screaming, they might have bluffed their way out. As it was . . ." Her voice trailed off, and she shivered a little.

The policeman picked up her story, rising to refill his coffee. "As it was, they made the mistake of trying to speed past the patrol car and ended up in the ditch."

"Tame as lambs, both of them," the other officer said genially. "There's nothing like crawling out of an overturned car into the hands of the police to tame a fellow down."

"You were lucky not to have been hurt back there, bounching around with those crates," the man told Shelley. The phones had been ringing steadily from the next room during their talk. A man came to the door and looked around. "Which one of you is Dana Morrison?" he asked.

Dana rose and looked down at herself. With the blanket off and her face rosy with warmth, she must look like a large, dirty clown. She held out the sides of the overall pants with her fingers and made a deep bow before following the man into the next room.

"Where are they now?" Faith asked. "The men who kidnapped Shelley, I mean."

"Safe behind bars, waiting to be picked up by the Boston police," he said comfortably. "For all they know they are also facing a murder charge. They said right off that a girl had fallen into the mill pond up there and frozen to death. You haven't asked about the paintings. We got them back safe, too."

"Paintings?" Faith asked. "What paintings?"

"Is that what was in the crates?" Shelley asked.

He nodded and rose. He unlocked a closet across the room and pulled out one of the familiar crates. "Want to see the big one?" he asked.

Even in the ordinary light of that room, the painting glowed with life.

Faith stared at the picture in disbelief. The girl in the painting looked no older than herself — fifteen, maybe sixteen. Her hair was long and very dark, in glowing ringlets. She wore a ring of bright red roses like a crown. From the loving way she was looking into the shawl in her lap you just knew that it held a child in its folds. All the light in the painting glowed from the unseen child. It lit the curves of the girl's face and caught the petals of the roses, deepening their perfection.

Faith heard Shelley's quick intake of breath. "*The Madonna of the Roses*," she said in a tone of whispered amazement. "Aunt Edie was right. It is magnificent! Is that the copy that Mr. and Mrs. Flint had stolen from them?"

Faith looked from Shelley back to the painting. "From what Mr. Flint told us, that probably isn't a copy but the original that was stolen from a European museum. That's what this whole miserable kidnapping has been about. This art thief was going to be tried on March the first, and they were trying to keep Mr. Flint from testifying against him."

"The first," Shelley whispered, remembering the voices behind the wall. The first. Of course, that meant the first of March. "And they thought I was Casey and that having me would keep him from testifying? They said they would be out of the country before anyone found me."

The sheriff's tone was wry. "I wouldn't say it was a textbook operation, but you kids sure put a stop to all that. And almost got one of you killed for your pains. They said right off that she was dead, the tall one in the baggy pants."

Faith smothered a laugh as Dana came to the door.

"Your turn, Faith," she said. "You're wanted on the telephone."

Faith expected to hear Mr. Flint's voice. Her mother's voice brought an instant lump to her throat.

"Oh, Mom," she said swiftly. "I'm so sorry. I thought we'd reach you before you found out we were gone."

"I just wanted to tell you that we are all here in Greenleaf, and Mr. Flint has sent a limousine for you kids. And I wanted you to know that I am so relieved that you are all right after behaving like such an absolute idiot." Her voice had risen dangerously with the last words. Then she caught herself, and her tone turned soft. "Your father would have been very proud of you." Then she briskly suggested that Faith call Shelley to the phone, "so that her parents can hear her voice with their own ears."

Faith had to stand by the phone a moment to regain her composure before calling Shelley.

With Bret's car off somewhere with its nose badly out of joint, he rode back to Boston in the limousine with them. He sat on the jump seat in the back, holding Dana's hand in his.

"I think I understand less of this than even Shelley did," he complained. "Can't somebody take it from the top for me?"

No wonder Dana was a straight *A* student in English. Faith listened to her explanation with real admiration.

When she finished explaining how Mr. Flint had innocently imported genuine works of art thinking they were copies, only to have them stolen, Bret whistled softly. "That's wild."

"Not so wild as their plan to keep Mr. Flint from testifying by kidnapping his daughter," Dana pointed out.

"But it almost worked," Bret reminded her. "They were trapped by one teeny little mistake — they took the wrong girl." He grinned. "I think I know how they must feel. This would have been a most successful wild day for me, except for one little mistake. Snow-plows are very expensive brakes."

Dana laughed and patted his hand.

"But they do make the most remarkable roadblocks to stop kidnappers and art thieves."

CHAPTER EIGHTEEN

Sometime during that long ago (or so it seemed) Parent-Alumnae Weekend, one of the graduates had told Dana about her wedding.

"We were married in the back parlor of the Inn," she explained. "He was from Oakley Prep, and I was a Canby Hall girl. He had gone on to Rutgers, and I to Barnard. But when we were ready to get married, we came back here."

Dana looked around the spacious old room, which she had never heard of before listening to that story. Upon hearing of Shelley's rescue and the triumphant return of *The Madonna of the Roses*, Mr. and Mrs. Flint had ordered a celebration supper for all of them at the Inn.

"After my shower and my hair washing and maybe another shower," Shelley said, when they told her what was planned.

Mr. Flint's party couldn't have had a prettier setting. The room was paneled halfway up with wood that shone in the candlelight. Faded hunting scenes decorated the upper walls, broken here and there by windows draped against the snowy night. Furniture had been moved aside to make room for a long buffet table, whose white cloth extended to the floor. The food was beautiful and arranged between giant candelabra. There was a huge ham with a cranberry glaze and garnish, a beef roast that curled pink under the serving knife, every fruit and vegetable imaginable, and great baskets of the famous Inn bread.

Someday Bret and I, Dana found herself thinking as she looked around the room. That was ridiculous, of course. It was silly even to think about your own wedding when you were fifteen, with as many dreams as she had. Still, if she were old enough to think about marriage, she would want these very people to be there. She would want Shelley, astonishingly thin in a full skirt and ruffled blouse, and Shelley's parents, who glowed with happiness by the big, deep fireplace. Dana's own mother was deep in conversation with Faith's mother and Mr. and Mrs. Flint. Casey was glued between her parents just as she had been that first night in Alison's penthouse.

And strangely, Casey looked more like

Shelley than ever. The difference was in her expression. She looked gentler, softer than Dana had ever seen her.

Bret was charming Alison, standing very tall to make up for the extra couple of inches in height that Alison had on him.

It took Dana a second to recognize the trim young man who stood at the door a moment, before walking directly toward her. Then she giggled.

"Oh, it's you," she said. "My favorite plumber."

"I understand that you have been seen in some pretty interesting costumes yourself lately." The FBI agent laughed. "I almost declined Mr. Flint's invitation to this party, but my curiosity wouldn't let me stay away."

Bret joined them and took Dana's hand.

"I was just getting ready to scold your girl," the agent explained when they had been introduced. "We really can't have you amateurs showing up the professionals like this."

"Don't give me any credit," Bret exclaimed. "I just went along for *their* ride."

"Bret," Dana protested. "In the end you saved the whole day."

"Tell me about the coded message," the agent urged. "Mr. Flint said it was something in that last call that sent you off on that wild snowy chase."

Dana motioned to Faith, who approached to shake hands with the agent.

"Faith is the one who broke the code," Dana explained.

"We have this game we all play together," Faith told him, explaining how it went.

He nodded thoughtfully. "I love my love with an *M*. Did you figure out at once that it was a mill?"

Faith shook her head. "That was the hardest one. But the *M* kept coming up." She smiled at him, her dark eyes glowing. "And did you ever know a fifteen-year-old who called her mother Mama-Millie? Especially if her mother's name is Ann?"

The agent laughed along with them.

"You don't happen to know what the Massachusetts law does to people who run into snowplows, do you?" Bret asked.

The agent laughed. "If what the sheriff told me about the condition of your car is correct, you're out of wheels for a while. But we have a phrase called 'mitigating circumstances.' I think recovering a kidnapped hostage and a stolen art treasure might make your offense fall into that category. We expect the trial Tuesday will put that pair away for a good long while."

"The man in the picture who was out at the mill, he was one of them, you know," Faith told him, still finding her skin a little prickly at the memory of the way he had thrown Shelley into the back of the van.

He nodded. "He was the idea man behind

the racket, we've learned. He got interested in the value of art when he was making crates for Mr. and Mrs. Flint. When he ran across a man who could make brilliant copies from originals, the plot was hatched. We feel very fortunate to have broken the ring before any of the originals disappeared into private collections. And with little more damage than a battered snowplow," he added to Bret.

"It sure stopped my horn," Bret laughed.

After the Flints' party was over, Alison Cavanaugh drove the three roommates back to Baker House. She was strangely quiet. Dana watched her warily from the corner of her eye.

Once inside, Alison turned to the three of them. "We still need to talk about this adventure in terms of Dana and Faith and the rules of Canby Hall."

Dana groaned inwardly. This was something she had known was coming but had shoved from her mind.

Alison's face was unreadable. She pushed her glasses up off her nose with her finger.

"You girls go change into your pajamas and meet me at my place at eleven sharp."

"What about me?" Shelley cried. "I want any punishment they get. Look what they did for me."

Alison looked at her thoughtfully. "Very well. All three of you. At eleven."

* * *

Shelley burst into tears the minute Alison left. Dana took her hand. "We'll be all right," she whispered earnestly. "Somehow we'll all be all right." Only to herself did she add, *We have to be!*

Promptly at eleven, they rapped on Alison's door. They could hear the soft strains of her stereo from inside and a faint meow from Doby. Then Alison opened the door.

Dana felt her stomach drop about a foot. Across the room, regal in a tailored suit with a pale silk blouse, stood Patrice Allardyce. Dana had never been this close to the headmistress of Canby Hall, except in passing during chapel.

All the things she had ever heard whispered about Patrice Allardyce flashed through her mind: That she had never been heard to laugh since some tragedy in her life. That her heart was pure ice just like her clear, pale eyes. That a broken Canby Hall rule was the same as high treason to her.

"Come in," Alison said.

Patrice Allardyce said nothing.

Alison waved the girls toward the deep cushions next to a couch. They sat down.

Patrice Allardyce remained standing.

Shelley, at Dana's side, seemed to be having some trouble breathing regularly. Faith sat so still that she might have been a work of art. If a leaf had fallen off one of Alison's plants onto the rug, you could have heard it.

Then, without warning, Patrice Allardyce began to speak.

"A Canby Hall girl is the pattern for all the fine things that a woman can and should be. Among these are loyalty, courage, and consideration for others. The days just passed have proved each of you in loyalty and courage. You have failed miserably in the third.

"The rules of Canby Hall are made for good reason. Only if they are broken for good reason can any infraction of them be forgiven. After a long conference with the investigators in charge of Michelle's abduction, I was convinced that they are not at all sure that they could have brought this case to a satisfactory close in time. They quite candidly confess that even if you had told them of the suspicious clues Michelle provided, they would have considered them too whimsical to follow up on.

"Based on those reasons, no punishment will be meted out for your infractions of the Canby Hall rules. We only require that this entire affair be kept secret from all who were not involved in it for the sake of the reputation of Canby Hall.

"That is all. Thank you very much and good night."

Dana was still trying to struggle to her feet to thank the headmistress when she was out of the door and gone.

Alison held up both hands and cautioned them to silence.

"Now if the three of you will please cover your eyes until I give you a count of five."

Dana heard Alison's quick steps back and forth and was consumed with curiosity. Doby liked whatever she was doing because he was mewing approval as he followed her back and forth.

"Five," she said.

Dana opened her eyes, gasped, and began to laugh.

"A rerun," Alison explained with delight. "Your mother planned it and brought the things, Dana. My only contribution is the cake."

The familiar coffee table was covered with food. Alison had set her toaster beside the bagels and cream cheese. The mustard that went with Faith's favorite giant pretzels was already perfuming the air. Shelley's peanut butter cookies with the chocolate kisses melted on top were piled daintily on a paper plate.

Right in the middle of all of it sat a birthday cake with four candles and a waggling line of frosting that spelled DANA.

When all of them were settled around the table on the floor pillows, Faith raised her glass of cola.

"A toast," she proposed. "I give you a toast."

With all the glasses up, Faith began:

"I love my love with an S because she is safely back home. Her name is Shelley and she lives in the shower. She eats Slime and Slide like it was superior stuff."

Dana closed her eyes to hold that moment of laughter in her mind forever — the three of them, happy like this, forever and ever.